"I don't know how to get down."

Kyle looked up at Maggie. "Well, why don't you just ease yourself off the branch and let go. I'll break your fall."

"Okay." And just like that, she jumped.

Kyle barely had time to brace himself before the impact, which carried them both to the ground. They lay there, chest to chest, panting in the purpling twilight. It was a position Kyle liked to be in with a woman. Especially this woman.

As feeling gradually returned to his extremities, he became aware of the silky curtain of her hair, Maggie's sweet smell and the soft weight of her body settled onto his. Her sweater had ridden up her rib cage and his hand was just below the edge.

Skin. Smooth, velvety skin.

Maggie propped herself off his chest, at the same time pressing her lower body into his. "I'm fine, in case you wondered," she said, easing off him.

Kyle gasped. Nothing was numb anymore, and in two seconds she'd know it. "You felt fine. In fact, you felt pretty damn good."

"After taking a trip to Georgia, I knew I had to write this book," admits **Heather MacAllister.** "And although I needed to do a lot of research into Southern customs, traditions, etc., the one thing I didn't need to research was the hero's profession. After all, most of the men in my family are engineers. In fact, when I described some of the scenes to my older son, he indignantly asked that I not put him into any more books!"

In February, 1998 be sure to watch for *Manhunting in Memphis,* Heather's contribution to Temptation's MANHUNTING miniseries. Hayley Parrish wins the wedding of her dreams— now she's got to find a groom! Don't miss the fun.

Books by Heather MacAllister

HARLEQUIN TEMPTATION

543—JILT TRIP
583—BEDDED BLISS
616—CHRISTMAS MALE
637—BRIDE OVERBOARD

LONG SOUTHERN NIGHTS
Heather MacAllister

Harlequin Books

TORONTO • NEW YORK • LONDON
AMSTERDAM • PARIS • SYDNEY • HAMBURG
STOCKHOLM • ATHENS • TOKYO • MILAN
MADRID • WARSAW • BUDAPEST • AUCKLAND

To the engineers in my life, who are
awfully nice to have around: my husband,
my father, my brother, my father-in-law
and my brother-in-law.

ISBN 0-373-25756-2

LONG SOUTHERN NIGHTS

Copyright © 1997 by Heather W. MacAllister.

Printed in U.S.A.

_____Prologue_____

"IF YOUR great-great-grandfather were alive to see this, it would kill him."

Maggie Jefferson's grandmother, Pearl, whose hair was as white as her name, peered through binoculars from atop a stepladder at the window of the second-best bedroom.

"Try not to let yourself get too upset," Maggie murmured soothingly, knowing that nothing she said would comfort her grandmother over the fact that a Yankee computer firm had built their new glass building on land Pearl had long ago decided should be a park honoring LaRue Jefferson, founder of Jeffersonville, Georgia.

"Oh! The Grants are there, too. Right in front! How _could_ they, after we had a pink tea for SaRita? Is there no loyalty? Add them to the list, Opal."

Tut-tutting, Maggie's great-aunt Opal dutifully listed the unfortunate Grants in a floral, clothbound notebook. The stepladder tilted as Pearl leaned forward to see which of her other soon-to-be former friends were attending the dedication of Stuart Park. She gasped.

"Careful, Grandmother," cautioned Maggie as she braced the stepladder.

"What's happening now, Pearl?" Opal's pink-cheeked face creased in concern.

"That puffed-up toad of a mayor is making a *speech*. Well, he can forget about us sponsoring his daughter. Mayor or not, he'll see just what kind of a marriage Lila can make without the backing of the Jeffersons of Jeffersonville. He's obviously forgotten that he wouldn't even *be* mayor if we hadn't generously overlooked the fact that he married a Nelson."

"Oh, is Paulina there?" Opal brightened.

"Right beside him on the dais."

"What's she wearing? Is it the blue dress, or did she buy the black-and-white-striped one like she said—"

"She looks like an awning," Pearl interrupted.

Smiling delightedly, Opal clapped her hands together, dropping her pencil and notebook in the process. "Diana wore that same ensemble on 'Lovers and Liars' last month," she said, referring to one of her favorite soap operas.

Slowly, Pearl lowered the binoculars to glare at her younger sister.

Opal's smile faded, and she retrieved her pencil and notebook.

Maggie had been the recipient of her grandmother's glacial stares before, and sent a sympathetic glance toward her great-aunt. "Do I hear something, Grandmother?"

Far in the distance, a strident rhythmic chanting threatened to drown out the mayor's speech. After a few tight-lipped seconds spent studying the scene through the binoculars, Pearl lowered them once more.

This time, Maggie was the recipient of Pearl's disapproving gaze. "It's your mother."

As though Maggie had any influence over her militantly feminist mother.

"What's Ruby doing?" Opal crowded Pearl and Maggie at the window and stood on her tiptoes. "Move over, Pearl. I can't see a thing." She tried to climb the stepladder, ignoring Pearl's outraged sputtering. "But it's *my* turn!"

"I can't bear to watch anymore, anyway." Pearl surrendered the binoculars and Opal eagerly ascended the stepladder.

Maggie continued to brace the ladder, hoping they'd soon lose interest in the park dedication and Stuart Computers' open house. She had to get started on her way to Atlanta. Tomorrow morning, she was to start her first job after graduation. But she didn't want her grandmother and great-aunt climbing the stepladder by themselves.

"This day will go down as one of the darkest in the Jefferson family history," Pearl declared.

"I can't see anything," Opal complained.

"With those vulgar false eyelashes, I'm not surprised."

"I'll have you know that these are the very same lashes worn by actresses of note, such as—"

"What's Mama doing?" Maggie asked, more to distract Opal than because she wanted to know.

Opal opened her false-lashed eyes wide and peered through the binoculars. "Picketing."

"*Is* she?" Pearl looked heavenward. "All my years of

trying to instill a sense of family honor in my only child have at last borne fruit. Ruby has raised her voice against that greedy Yankee—"

"She's demanding that the mayor keep his promise to build a battered women's shelter," Opal reported. "At least that's what her sign says."

"What about the travesty of naming that park for a Yankee?"

"No...nothing about the park."

Pearl sank onto a white wicker chair, which creaked in protest. Fanning herself with Opal's notebook, she eyed Maggie. "With Ruby for a mother, it's no wonder you're leaving the bosom of your family."

"And without a young man," Opal offered softly.

"Well, we wouldn't want Magnolia leaving with a young man, now, would we?" Pearl raised her eyebrows. "When she leaves, it should be with her *husband*."

Maggie's current state of being well-educated, but unwed, had been a constant source of friction. Though she loved the three women who'd raised her, it was time—past time—for her to move out of her rambling ancestral home and make her own way in the world. "And how do you know that I *don't* have a young man?" she asked.

"If you do, he isn't the right one," Pearl stated.

Opal was nodding in rare agreement. "That's right, dear. You don't have that glow."

And as long as she continued to live in this house, Maggie suspected she'd never find anybody to glow *with*.

The sounds of applause and cheering indicated that the dedication was just about over, but Opal and Pearl continued to study the crowd and list the names of those who'd failed to join them in their boycott of the ceremony. The exact method of retribution would no doubt occupy them for weeks to come, Maggie thought.

Footsteps sounded on the stairs. "Mama?"

"I thought you'd be long gone by now." Maggie's mother opened the hall-closet door and set the picket sign inside. It joined others from which Ruby could select a slogan for her cause *du jour*.

"Don't encourage her, Ruby," Pearl said.

"And why not?" Ruby strode into the bedroom and relieved Maggie of her post at the stepladder. "Maggie should learn to support herself so she'll never have to be dependent on a man."

"But men can be so...manly...." Sighing, Opal trailed off.

Pearl took back the binoculars. "She should stay in Jeffersonville and take her rightful place in society—"

Maggie had heard it all before. It was time to leave. "Goodbye, everyone!" she sang. "I've got to be going now."

"This instant?"

"Yes, Grandmother."

"But you'll miss tea!" Opal cried.

"I'll be back in a few weeks for the Fourth of July parade." She hugged the three women.

"After *this*, how can the parade ever be the same?"

Pearl fretted. "They'll probably ask that *Yankee* to be Uncle Sam!"

Ruby cackled. "Or maybe they'll let him play the part of LaRue Jefferson."

"*Ruby!*"

Maggie slipped from the room, eternally grateful to Mr. Stuart of Stuart Computers. With such a threat to the prominence of the Jefferson name to occupy them, the women wouldn't be interfering with Maggie's new life in Atlanta.

She was free, at last.

1

Six years later

"MR. MATSUZAKA, please accept my most humble apologies." Kyle Stuart simultaneously captured the attention of a hovering waiter and sent his hardware-development vice president a start-groveling look.

"What?" Mitchell McCormick, the brilliant but oblivious head of hardware development for Stuart Computers, stopped chewing.

Kyle directed a significant look at the dripping Mr. Matsuzaka and another at Mitch's elbow, which had sent a carafe of sake splashing into the lap of their host.

"Oh, hey—did I do that?"

Kyle nodded and raised his eyebrows, prompting Mitch for an apology.

"I didn't even feel it. Sorry." Mitch gazed at the mess and resumed chewing.

Kyle had hoped for more than an ungracious mumble through a mouthful of food.

A stone-faced Mr. Matsuzaka, now reeking of sake, allowed the waiter to dab at his shirtfront. "Please forgive me for placing the sake so close to your elbow."

Mitchell swallowed. "No problem." He stabbed the thinly sliced beef on his plate with the fork he'd insisted upon and shoved it into his mouth. "This stuff is great."

Kyle grimaced. Would this meal never end? Mitch was acting out every ugly-American cliché in the book and a few he'd come up with on his own.

With a sinking feeling, Kyle glanced around the other tables, noting how his upper management interacted with their reserved Japanese hosts.

Just this morning, Kyle had stressed the importance of tonight's dinner. After all, Matsuzaka Engineering had invited a dozen of Kyle's key executives to meet with them in San Francisco. Even though it meant flying everyone from Jeffersonville, Kyle welcomed the opportunity. Matsuzaka wouldn't have invited them if he wasn't seriously considering a joint venture with Kyle's company. Kyle knew the Japanese liked to meet more than half a dozen times to get to know prospective business associates and he hoped this dinner marked the prelude to a long and profitable corporate relationship.

He'd assumed his upper management would be on their best—meaning, conservatively formal—behavior.

They apparently didn't have a best behavior.

He didn't even want to consider that this might *be* their best behavior.

Why hadn't he noticed that socially, Mitch and the others were a little rough around the edges? The engineers preferred their computers to people, but this was business. Did they act this way when they met with clients on their own?

The tension in the room grew. The Matsuzaka people were graciously reserved and the Stuart engineers became even more awkward and ill at ease, perhaps sensing that something was wrong and not knowing what it was. Conversation was nonexistent.

Mitch was the worst of the lot. Kyle tried mental telepathy. Staring so hard his eye muscles hurt, he willed Mitch to look at him. Deftly handling a pair of mother-of-pearl chopsticks, he brought a small piece of the velvety marbled meat to his mouth and savored it.

Mitch chomped on, preparing to eat the last mouthful on his plate.

"Would you care for more?" inquired Mr. Matsuzaka.

"No, thank you," Kyle said at once. *Mitch, say no, thank you.*

"That'd be great!" Mitch enthusiastically handed his plate to the waiter.

Their host inclined his head.

Kyle gave thoughtful and serious consideration to strangling Mitchell McCormick.

Instead, he faced Mr. Matsuzaka and smiled the patented wide smile that had rarely failed to charm anyone, and prepared to salvage the rest of the evening.

His efforts were sabotaged by Mitch. "Best steak I've ever eaten."

"I made special arrangements for my honored guests," Mr. Matsuzaka pronounced as Mitch accepted another stark white plate with thin slices of beef fanning around the edge.

"Kobe beef is a delicacy in Japan, Mitch." Kyle gave

the word *delicacy* a subtle emphasis which he hoped Mitch would hear and his hosts would not.

"Wonnurful," Mitch said through a mouthful of the one-hundred-and-fifty-dollar-a-pound beef. "Do they have doggie bags here? Slather on a little hot mustard, and this would make a killer sandwich."

Kyle winced.

At last, Mitch's enormous capacity for expensive beef was satisfied.

Kyle's attempts to charm Mr. Matsuzaka had been rewarded by a smile or two, and he began to hope that this might lead to the long-awaited contract with the Japanese company.

"So, hey, let's get down to business." Mitch pushed the plate aside and fumbled through his leather bomber jacket, impatiently loosening the tie he'd been forced to wear to comply with the restaurant's dress code.

"This has been such an enjoyable evening. Let's save business for another time," Kyle suggested, hoping Mitch would realize it wasn't a suggestion at all. The Japanese hated to rush business.

"Huh?" Mouth hanging open, Mitch gazed at Kyle.

In Mitch's eyes, Kyle saw the first inkling that his vice president perceived all was not well, or at least that's what he *thought* he saw. But when Mitch pulled a palm-top computer out of his jacket pocket, Kyle knew he was in trouble. Mitch was dense. "I can calculate the conversion-cost figures for each memory chip right now."

If they hadn't been sitting on the floor, Kyle would have reached under the table and kicked him.

No, that probably would be too subtle for Mitch.

"Let's wait until we get back to Jeffersonville," Kyle said, smoothly confiscating Mitch's toy.

"We are interested in visiting your manufacturing facilities," stated Mr. Matsuzaka.

He was? Swallowing his astonished relief, Kyle dared to hope that the evening hadn't been a complete failure. "It would be my pleasure to show you around Stuart Computers and to have the opportunity for you to be our guests when your schedule permits." Behind his smile, Kyle held his breath.

Mr. Matsuzaka leaned toward his advisers for a discreet conference.

Mitch sulked over the loss of his computer. Fine, as long as he sulked silently.

Kyle sipped his tea and pretended that nothing much was at stake, certainly not his chance of being the first computer firm to offer the leading-edge, ten-gigabit memory chip.

Being first with the most was everything. In the past two years, Stuart Computers' new business had dropped off dramatically. Kyle knew he had a high-quality product at an equitable price, but competition was greater than it had been the year Kyle had raided his college fund and he, Mitch and two other buddies had begun the company.

Back then, business had come to them. Now they had to court new markets. And they were losing out.

After eight years of astonishing growth, Stuart Computers was coasting and Kyle thought he'd finally figured out why. His entire upper management was under the age of thirty. They were competing against seasoned executives who'd been in business since before the Stuart management had been born. Youthful enthusiasm could no longer hold its own with polished professionalism.

But if he had an exclusive contract to use this memory chip, his team could be as raw and unpolished as they pleased, and no one would care. The simple fact was that the company who got this chip first would blow the competition out of the water, and Kyle's survival depended on being first.

The huddled conference had ended. "We would be pleased to visit your plant in June."

Three months away. Kyle almost groaned aloud. That meant Matsuzaka had other companies under consideration. But at least Stuart Computers was one of them. "We'll look forward to your visit."

"And we will look forward to seeing the charming Jeffersonville of which you have spoken so highly." Mr. Matsuzaka smiled. "It is good when a community and a business live in harmony."

"Harmony?"

"Yes. We have no wish to offend the community. Many of our people will be living there."

"Most of my employees also live in Jeffersonville. I can't imagine them being offended at anything which is for the good of the company."

"Excellent. To be the source of...antagonism is distasteful to us." Matsuzaka's people murmured in agreement. He held up a hand and there was immediate silence. "We noted the difficulties experienced by Fuyiko when they built their manufacturing plant in a small town. Their presence caused such offense that the Fuyiko families could not remain. It was a failure." His head bowed slightly.

And such a failure would be intolerable. Mr. Matsuzaka didn't need to tell Kyle that.

So, essentially, what Mr. Matsuzaka *was* telling him was that the community where he would locate was equally as, if not more, important than, the computer company they would select.

He was doomed.

His engineers could be coached, but there was no harmony in Jeffersonville. Somehow, he'd alienated Pearl Jefferson, grande dame of Jeffersonville society. Just because he couldn't trace his family back to anybody who'd founded anything didn't give her the right to treat him and his employees like dirt. But she had.

Fortunately, being a society leader wasn't important to Kyle. He'd only applied to join the Jeffersonville Country Club because it seemed to be expected. When he'd been denied membership, he knew it was because of her.

He'd tried to call her after that, but she wasn't "at home," so he'd stopped making the attempt.

Frankly, Pearl Jefferson's small-town snobbery hadn't affected him at all—until now.

THE HEAVY GLASS DOORS of Drake Office Supply whooshed closed behind Maggie Jefferson, closing the door on her career in sales, as well.

Of course she hadn't made any sales, so she supposed her week-long stint at Drake didn't count. In a way, Maggie was relieved to have been fired. She'd hated sales ever since she'd tried to peddle Girl Scout cookies, which was probably why she hadn't been any good at it. And, too, most of the merchants in Jeffersonville knew her or her family, and couldn't quite see "that charming Miss Jefferson" as a salesperson.

Unfortunately, they couldn't see her as an employee, either. Everyone naturally assumed that Maggie Jefferson, direct descendant of Jeffersonville's founder, wanted to work for the fun of it. The problem with having a town named after your great-great-grandfather, she thought as she walked toward the car, was that everyone automatically believed that fame and wealth went hand in hand.

There was wealth in the town of Jeffersonville, Georgia, but it wasn't in the hands of the Jefferson family. And Maggie had been fruitlessly trying to correct the situation ever since she discovered the genteel way of life enjoyed by her mother, grandmother and great-aunt was threatened by a lack of funds.

As she reached the end of the tree-lined street and turned the corner into the parking lot, the sun flashed off the towering glass Stuart Computers building.

Jeffersonville natives hated the modern structure and the newcomers who'd moved in to work there, though Maggie had always thought the landscaped grounds and park were a vast improvement on the tangled thatch of the old Holcombe place, which had previously occupied that address.

Now, *that's* where the jobs are, she thought. Too bad her grandmother was being so hardheaded about letting Maggie apply for one there. After all, the Yankee-owned company had been in Jeffersonville for nearly six years. They weren't going to go away, no matter how long her grandmother continued to snub them. And as for the park, why *shouldn't* it have been named after the man who'd paid for it?

Oh, what was the use? After the way her family had acted toward anyone who dared associate with Stuart personnel, she'd never make it past the receptionist anyway.

She had a master's in business administration and had worked for a company in nearby Atlanta as a corporate-personnel trainer until it had downsized last fall. One would think she'd have no trouble finding a job. But one would be wrong, and now finances had forced her to move back home, only to discover that the finances there were worse.

Returning home meant returning to the stifling way of life Maggie had tried to escape. It was amazing how quickly she'd settled back into the patterns of her girlhood. One raised eyebrow from her grandmother, and Maggie had stopped wearing short skirts, instead adopting the long florals that met with her grandmother's approval. Unfortunately, they weren't business-like, but the townspeople didn't accept her in her business suits, either.

After climbing into her grandmother's pink antique

Cadillac, Maggie slammed the door shut, enjoying the loud sound, but missing the flashy import she'd had to sell.

Some businesswoman she was, not even realizing how much the family fortune had shrunk. The signs had all been there, but she hadn't wanted to see them. She'd just assumed... But it was too late now.

Maggie rested her head on the steering wheel. Being ladylike, sweet and nice—in other words, upholding the Jefferson image—wasn't going to pay the bills. People seemed to expect the Jefferson women to sit around in white gloves and hold tea parties all day long—probably because that was precisely the impression her grandmother fostered.

Maggie, alone among the Jefferson women, was truly aware of their precarious financial position. And she, alone among the Jefferson women, was going to have to do something about it. After all, they couldn't support themselves on charm alone, could they?

Or could they?

MITCH PACED AROUND Kyle's office in agitation. "We've been together since the beginning and you always said you'd handle the people stuff and leave the computers to me. Right?"

"Right." Kyle rubbed his temple, trying to head off the monster headache he felt coming on. Stuart Computers might not survive the coming visit by the Japanese. "Since you're one of Stuart's founders, Matsuzaka will think it strange, even insulting, if you aren't attending any of the entertainments."

"Then he can just be insulted," Mitch said.

Kyle gazed sightlessly at the newspaper on his desk. Mitch was, and always would be, Mitch. Although he was a vice president, and a twenty-eight-year-old millionaire, he looked and acted like the precocious and introverted college freshman he'd been when Kyle had first met him. Over the years, Kyle had accepted his friend's idiosyncrasies, but the disastrous dinner with the Japanese had shown him others might not.

"You can't avoid business socializing forever, Mitch. I can give you a few pointers on how to act. Or we could ask someone else to coach you."

"I don't need coaching! Anyway, I'm not into that etiquette stuff." Mitch waved a hand. "Bunch of stupid rules. Just count me out of any more fancy-schmancy dinners."

Kyle tilted his chair back. "Can't do that."

"Now wait a minute—"

"In the next three months, Matsuzaka and his team will visit each of the companies they're considering for this venture. They want to see Jeffersonville and how happy we all are. So while they're here, we'll entertain them and show them the town and a little of Atlanta. Let them know they'll be welcome here. In the process, we'll be selling them on Stuart Computers and showing them the wonderful relationship we have with the community." Kyle paused to let his words sink in, hoping that by the time the Japanese arrived, they'd be true.

Mitch shoved his hands into his pockets and stared down at his tennis shoes. "Selling is Lane's job. I never had to do that before. I don't *want* to do it. I want to design."

Kyle gritted his teeth. "Getting the chip depends on this visit, Mitch."

"The Japanese wouldn't matter if you'd leave me alone and let me design my own ten-gig chip."

Kyle spoke slowly. "Matsuzaka already has the chip. Whoever uses it corners the market. Everyone else will play catch-up."

Mitch pouted. His irritation with anything that took him away from his beloved computers was legendary. "Well, then, let them talk to Pat."

"Pat's in applications."

"The Japanese don't have to know that."

Kyle knew he couldn't get through to his friend. Mitch was, and probably always would be, a living stereotype of a computer engineer. He wore polyester pants, tennis shoes and a shirt with a pocket protector that had failed to protect against leaky engineering pens and India ink. He needed a haircut and, so help him, was sporting electrical tape around his glass frames.

"Why don't you buy new frames for your glasses?" Kyle asked impulsively. "You can certainly afford it."

Mitch shrugged. "The primary function of correctional lenses is to increase vision acuity. These work."

Kyle grimaced.

"What? You think that Matsuzaka will notice my glasses?" Mitch's voice was shrilly defensive.

"Calm down, Mitch." Mitch might be socially oblivious, but he could be hurt. Easily. "We can talk again when I've made a few plans."

"Well, don't include me in any plans," Mitch warned, just before he loped out of the office.

Kyle closed his door so he could be alone to think. Between the Jefferson woman and Mitch, he had a lot to contemplate. By himself, Mitch could be considered eccentric—but the others were just as bad. And without Mitch's full cooperation, the others wouldn't bother to learn to be socially adept either. They simply didn't believe socializing was important.

To Pearl Jefferson, social order was everything. If she were the only one snubbing him, he could call her an eccentric, too. But, as with Mitch, without her cooperation, the town wouldn't follow.

Kyle fingered this morning's *Jeffersonville Journal* and flipped to the insert that had caught his attention. Jeffersonville's First Family Offers Charm School, read the headline. The article announced the start of coed classes taught by Maggie Jefferson, direct descendant of LaRue Jefferson, founder of Jeffersonville.

The Jeffersons were offering etiquette lessons. Kyle's executives needed etiquette lessons. They should be able to get together on this.

But how could they? Kyle couldn't change the fact that he'd been born a Yankee and that was the only reason he could think of that made the Jeffersons hate him so much. If they knew that losing out on the new memory chip might force him to sell the building and cut his workforce, they'd be thrilled.

Stubborn females. Couldn't they see that without a

major business in town, all the young people would leave for Atlanta and points beyond? Not everyone was born wealthy. Some people had to work for a living. There was no shame in it.

He linked his fingers behind his head and propped his feet on the desk. He'd never met Maggie Jefferson and wondered whether she was as starched-up as her grandmother, or a reasonable woman who'd agree to conduct classes for Mitch and the others.

Yes, Maggie Jefferson was the key. If she could do the job, hiring her would be a way to enlist the grandmother's cooperation. The Japanese visit would be like a final exam and the Jefferson School of Charm would want their pupils to pass, wouldn't they? This could work. It could really work.

It was all going to depend on the approach. What if Miss Jefferson couldn't do the job? Kyle would have to fire her and bring in an outside firm. Just the thought of the fallout from that made him shudder.

No, he'd have to test her without her knowing she was being tested. After this morning's conversation with his vice president, there was no way Mitch would go to them, and Pearl Jefferson would slam the door in Kyle's face. She might slam the door in Mitch's face, too, but at least he'd have a better chance.

Slowly, Kyle sat up and dropped his feet to the floor. That was it. *He* could meet Maggie Jefferson by pretending to *be* Mitch—Mitch at his most socially inept. The more Kyle thought about it, the more he liked the idea. This way, if things didn't work out, the Jeffersons would never know Kyle had contacted them.

Perfect.

"MAGNOLIA, DEAR, have some iced tea." Pearl perched a mint sprig on the lip of a tall glass.

"Thank you, Grandmother." Maggie accepted the glass and took a long swallow. It was one of the warmest springs on record and she'd spent the entire day outside tramping all over downtown Jeffersonville, or what was left of Jeffersonville. In the years since Atlanta had sprawled toward them, most businesses had closed down or moved into the city until the much-hated Stuart Computers arrived. Pearl would faint if she knew Maggie had actually left flyers for the charm school in the lobby of the Stuart building.

Slumping on the chintz sofa, she closed her eyes and enjoyed the breeze from the ceiling fan.

Attendance at afternoon tea was mandatory. Pearl was waiting for Maggie's grandfather to return from the war. World War II. Even though it was determined that her wartime husband had run off with a Parisian chanteuse, Pearl insisted that he would return eventually, and when he did, she didn't want him to find her unprepared.

Somehow, Pearl had decided that he would arrive in the afternoon. Thus, she prepared tea daily and insisted that everyone present themselves, properly attired, calmly awaiting the repentant prodigal's return.

"Sit up, Magnolia." Sighing inwardly, Maggie complied. Maggie's grandmother was the only one who called her Magnolia. It wasn't that she hated her name, at least not anymore, but Magnolia Blossom Jefferson wasn't a name people let pass without comment.

"Harlan Edwards proved to be a severe disappointment," her grandmother stated, referring to Maggie's former boss at Drake Office Supply. "Though I shouldn't be at all surprised. He *is* a man."

Maggie's losing her job had provided the topic of conversation at afternoon tea for the past week. "I think Mr. Edwards counted on the Jefferson name to impress his clients," Maggie suggested, weary of rehashing the subject.

"As well it should," stated her grandmother. "I'd assumed he wanted to hire you in an executive capacity. Imagine, a Jefferson being forced to go hat in hand—"

"I think Maggie should sue for discrimination." Ruby Jefferson stabbed a needle into her quilt.

"Mama!"

"He gave your job to a man, didn't he? One who went behind your back and stole your customers."

"I never made a sale. I didn't have any customers," Maggie protested, annoyed at having to defend both Mr. Edwards and the aggressive salesman to whom she'd lost her job.

"I intend to investigate the number of females in the Drake sales force." Her mother paused in her quilting. She gazed into the distance, the light of a new battle for women's rights in her eyes. "I imagine that the Equal Employment Opportunity Commission would be interested."

"Mama, please. I don't want my job back. Besides, if

Mr. Edwards thinks the Jefferson name is worth something, then it ought to be worth something to us."

The light faded from Ruby's eyes. "Are you referring to your idea of starting up Salina Garthwhiddle's School of Manners?"

"Yes," Maggie confirmed. "Jeffersonville hasn't had a charm school since she died." Reaching for a thin lemon cookie, Maggie munched and defended her plans. Again. "I've got experience in personnel training and conducting seminars. I'm not a secretary or a salesclerk or a receptionist—or an office-supply representative. I've already planned the curriculum and I took all the breakables out of the front parlor."

"Etiquette represses women," muttered Ruby darkly.

"Nonsense, Ruby." Pearl dropped a cube of sugar into her tea. Unlike Maggie and her mother, Pearl drank hot tea, no matter what the weather. "Much of the trouble in this world is caused by rudeness. If everyone would be polite to one another, we'd never have to fight another silly war."

Like the one you're fighting with the Stuart people? But of course Maggie didn't say it aloud. She didn't dare get Pearl started on the "Yankee blight" afflicting the Jeffersonville community.

"Atlanta has several etiquette schools," Maggie said, instead. "And why should Jeffersonville parents drive their children all the way into Atlanta when I'm perfectly capable of teaching them everything they need to know here?"

"With *our* help, of course," her grandmother said,

obliquely implying that Maggie's own manners needed careful scrutiny.

As Ruby bent over her quilt, her long gray-streaked hair fell over her shoulders. "I don't see any pupils."

Maggie bit her tongue.

"You did mention that we're the descendants of LaRue Jefferson, founder of Jeffersonville?" Pearl straightened with unconscious pride.

"Yes, but everyone already knows that, Grandmother." Actually, there had been inquiries about the school, but when people discovered that the descendants of LaRue Jefferson were charging tuition, interest in the charm school dropped off. Maggie had carefully concealed this from her grandmother, since she'd also concealed the fact that she intended to charge tuition. Her grandmother chose to believe that Maggie was merely occupying her time in a ladylike way until she attracted an eligible suitor.

Maggie thought she just might scream.

"Well, if people were desperate to learn what Salina Garthwhiddle had to teach, then they should be grateful to us." Pearl sniffed. "Salina always put on airs, even though the Garthwhiddles were no more than shabby genteel."

"It probably took Miss Garthwhiddle a while to become established," Maggie said, wondering exactly how long. They needed income right away. Her attention was caught by the heavy silver tea service her grandmother used every afternoon. Picking up the sugar bowl, she hefted it in her hand. This piece alone might bring enough to fix that pesky leak in the second-best upstairs guest room.

"Maybe we could sell this," she murmured, unaware that she'd spoken aloud until she heard her grandmother's horrified, "Magnolia! We will *never* sell your great-great-grandmother's silver! This house, and everything in it, is a sacred trust."

The sacred trust was crumbling around their ears. "It was just a thought." And an idea she'd keep in mind if the charm school didn't work out, Maggie decided, replacing the sugar bowl.

"And one of your poorer ones, just like you hunting for work when that company in Atlanta no longer needed you to teach their employees," her grandmother pronounced. Maggie always wondered why her former job wasn't considered "work." "Magnolia, I can't begin to tell you how distressed I was at the thought of you employed as a common salesperson." She dropped her voice as she said the word and darted a glance to the small sitting room adjacent to the main parlor.

"Yes, you can and you have. Every morning." Maggie's mother snipped her sewing thread.

"She should have chosen something else out of respect for Opal's feelings. Losing her job was divine retribution."

Maggie felt that scream coming on. "Aunt Opal never said a word."

"And she wouldn't. But she suffered, oh, how she suffered." Pearl averted her face and Maggie heard a sniff.

Laughter sounded from the next room, where Maggie's great-aunt Opal watched television.

"She's not suffering now," Ruby commented.

"You would begrudge your aunt any small pleasure she could wring out of life after her past...disappointment?" Pearl challenged significantly.

"I'm sure Cousin Coral will be interested to hear that she's a disappointment."

Pearl spoke in a harsh whisper. "I was not referring to dear Coral, but the *circumstances* of her conception."

Ruby shrugged as she measured another length of thread. "So the salesman was disappointing in the sack. Don't blame it on Maggie."

"Ruby Jefferson." Pearl trained horrified blue eyes on her daughter. "Child of my loins..."

"Stop it, both of you!" Maggie jumped to her feet. This endless bickering between her mother and grandmother was driving her nuts. Ruby had failed in her attempt to break with the strong southern traditions espoused by Pearl. Pearl had never forgiven her for the attempt and Ruby had never forgiven herself for failing. They'd taken their conflict out on Maggie, with Ruby preaching independence and Pearl preaching tradition.

"I refuse to believe I lost my job because of divine retribution for reminding Aunt Opal that she was seduced—"

"Magnolia Blossom Jefferson! I won't have that word spoken in this house!"

At the sound of her full name, Maggie gritted her

teeth and amended her word choice. "That her *virtue was stolen* by a traveling salesman over forty years ago!"

"A lady never recovers from the theft of her virtue."

"Mama," Ruby inserted, "I recovered."

"That's because you gave yours away."

"Grandmother!"

Ruby's reply was never uttered, because at that precise moment, the doorbell sounded.

All talking ceased as the three women stared at the front door.

"Magnolia, it appears we have a caller." Her grandmother carefully arranged herself in the needlepoint-covered chair at the head of the tea table, her hands folded in her lap. With a nod of her white head, she signaled Maggie to open the door.

Maggie wished she didn't have to go through this little charade every time the doorbell rang unexpectedly. She hated seeing the masked disappointment in her grandmother's eyes.

"Ruby, dear, don't slouch."

Maggie's mother straightened. In spite of Ruby's objections, Maggie's father was considered a possible visitor. Frankly, Maggie wouldn't know him even if he showed up on the doorstep. He and her mother had separated before Maggie's birth.

The television blared. Without being told, Maggie stopped by to alert her aunt Opal to join the tableau. It was hoped that after the Disgrace, the traveling salesman who'd deserted Opal might see the error of his ways and return with honorable intentions. Opal, impeccably coiffed and dressed in soap-opera-chic attire, immediately turned off the TV, joined her family in the next room and took her place on the settee opposite Pearl.

A caller arriving during the precise time her grandmother thought her years of devotion would be rewarded was rare, but not unheard of, and Maggie found her anticipation building.

There were times—times she was not proud to acknowledge—when she hoped the caller might be for her. A knight in shining armor, or the modern equivalent in a well-cut business suit, who'd whisk her away and solve all her problems. And he could be wealthy and she wouldn't hold it against him.

Get a grip, she admonished herself, opening the door.

Blue eyes blinked at her from behind thick, black-framed glasses. "Is this the Jefferson School of Charm?"

"Yes, it is," she responded, noting the polyester beltless pants with little snagged threads waving in the breeze, the tennis shoes, the short-sleeved shirt and the pocket protector. She sighed. The glasses even had broken frames. No one dressed like that anymore. It was a joke. Another person making fun of them.

"Well, then—" the man before her opened his arms wide "—charm me!" He laughed.

At least Maggie assumed the hiccuping donkey noise coming from him was laughter.

"Good day," she said in her most charming voice, and shut the door.

The bell rang at once.

Reluctantly, Maggie opened the door again. She'd suffered crank calls, but until now, at least no one had harassed her in person.

"I came about this," he said, thrusting one of her flyers in front of her face.

Maggie automatically stepped backward, which the stranger apparently mistook for an invitation to enter.

"Did you wish to inquire about classes for your children?" If the man's children were anything like him, Maggie's first etiquette class would go into overtime.

"Hell, no, pardon my French." More donkey hiccups.

Maggie edged down the hall, nearer the drawing room.

The man edged after her until they appeared in the doorway. "I want to 'learn the gentle art of social discourse,'" he said, quoting from the flyer. "I want to 'feel confident in social settings...overcome my fear of cutlery and facilitate my relations with persons of the opposite gender.'"

Maggie winced. Read aloud, Opal's writing was a bit flowery. The whole idea had been to foster the impression of genteel southern ways.

"Magnolia, have you a gentleman caller?" Pearl waited expectantly.

"Uh, no. Well, yes, but—"

"You may present him to us."

Great. The instructor had to be reminded of her manners. What a wonderful impression she was making.

"Grandmother, this is—" *This is absurd.* "This gentleman is inquiring about enrolling in our school."

"What is the gentleman's name?"

"We haven't got that far," Maggie said, exasperated to have lost control.

"The name's Mitchell McCormick."

Mitchell McCormick lurched forward and grabbed Pearl's hand, pumping it up and down. He released it, grabbed Opal's, pumped it, too, and reached for Ruby's. She glared and brandished her quilting needle.

Momentarily at a loss, he stepped back.

Unfortunately, the tea table was directly behind him.

"Mr. McCormick!" Maggie grabbed for the pitcher of iced tea and whisked it away.

The tray of lemon cookies and the silver tea service did not fare as well.

Mitchell, wearing an expression of comical surprise, vainly tried to keep his balance, but ultimately crashed across the table and landed, along with the lemon cookies, at Maggie's feet.

A gaping Maggie met a pair of rueful blue eyes. Blue. They *would* have to be blue. She'd discovered a weakness for blue eyes.

And they were intelligent blue. His glasses had slipped down the bridge of his nose and she was struck how, even prostrate at her feet, he managed a certain attraction.

"Magnolia," her grandmother mused into the silence, "I believe we shall accept Mr. McCormick as a *private* pupil."

2

FLAT ON HIS FACE in front of Pearl Jefferson, just where she'd always wanted him, Kyle pondered his predicament. He hadn't meant to make such a vivid impression. On the other hand, he was in like Flynn. Or Mitch was. He'd deal with that detail later.

What he was dealing with now was Maggie Jefferson, specifically, the unintended view he had of her legs. They matched his general impression, fogged slightly by Mitch's extra set of glasses, that Maggie was a babe. She had longish, thick, lush hair, and a knowing look that she didn't get from the human heirlooms sitting on the couch.

How come no one had ever told him about Maggie Jefferson? Kyle had thought he'd met all the eligible females in town—their mothers had seen to it.

Maggie wasn't wearing a wedding ring, just a sedate garnet on her right hand.

Their future collaboration now seemed loaded with delightful side benefits.

A pointed throat-clearing broke into his thoughts.

"Oh. I'm okay." He hopped to his feet and brushed powdered sugar from Mitch's pants. "No problem."

"How fortunate that the antique silver tea service broke your fall," Pearl murmured dryly.

"It's seen worse, Grandmother," Maggie said.

"Yes, it was threatened by the Yankees that time, too." Pearl glared at him.

Inwardly, Kyle was suffering agonies of indecision. He owed these women an apology, but Mitch would probably make some comment about the table being in the way. "Well, thank you, Mrs. Jefferson, for accepting me into your charm school."

"Classes will be taught by my granddaughter, Magnolia."

Magnolia. What a name. Kyle couldn't help glancing at her.

She wore a carefully blank look that told him making a comment about her name would be a fatal error, jeopardizing not only their future working relationship, but torpedoing a personal one, as well.

They locked gazes for a few moments, then Maggie knelt and began picking up the cookies.

Kyle immediately bent to help her, causing threads in the seams of the polyester-knit pants to audibly break.

"Magnolia, you'll want to inform Mr. McCormick of the arrangements for his classes."

"Oh, yeah, I can't wait to come back." And he popped one of the lemon cookies into his mouth.

Mr. MITCHELL McCORMICK was obviously pleased with his status as a private pupil.

Miss Maggie Jefferson was not. She'd seen the satisfied gleam in his eye. This man was obviously making fun of her and her family and she refused to tolerate it.

Jeffersonville considered the Jefferson women eccentric, old-fashioned and proud, but they were Maggie's family and she loved them.

It was too bad about Mitchell McCormick. Anyone who would derive amusement from mocking them needed all the etiquette he could get.

She thought about what she was going to say as she led him out of sight of the ruined afternoon-tea tableau. When they reached the spacious foyer of the old house, she spun around, the full skirt of her floral-print dress billowing around her.

"Mr. McCormick—"

"Call me Mitch. And I'll call you Magnolia, is it?"

"You can call me Miss Jefferson."

He stepped toward her. "Oh, but I much prefer Magnolia."

"And I prefer Maggie." She forced herself to remain in one spot rather than begin their back-stepping dance once again.

"Maggie it is, then." His lips stretched in a wide, smooth grin. A little too wide. A little too smooth.

Maggie gave him a long, direct look. "That's not the way it works," she said quietly. "But I suspect you know that already, don't you?"

His wide grin shrank, the gleam in his eyes dulled. "I apologize, Miss Jefferson."

He looked contrite. Sincerely contrite. Appealingly contrite.

She'd always been a sucker for true remorse. Perhaps she'd misjudged him. "Call me Maggie," she offered with a faint smile, aware that her grandmother would frown on such familiarity.

"Maggie." He shoved his hands into his pockets and tilted his head to one side, studying her from behind dark-framed glasses. "And I've already asked you to call me Mitch. Not that I know whether or not you will," he murmured.

He was an interesting mix of goofiness and self-assurance. "Where do you work?" she asked impulsively.

He hesitated so slightly, she almost didn't notice it. "Stuart Computers."

Of course. The man was obviously an engineer. Where else would he work?

He rocked back on his heels. If he'd been wearing suspenders, she imagined he would have gripped them. "I'm the vice president."

"I see." What she saw was that he was still playing her for a fool. "I hope you enjoyed your little game." Walking past him, Maggie opened the door. "Good day, Mr. McCormick."

"Wait—when do classes start?"

Maggie glared at him. "What is this, a bet? A fraternity prank? A slow news day? Are you a reporter who'll make fun of us in print?"

"No." He actually looked shocked. "Does that happen to you a lot?"

"More than to most people." Maggie gazed over his shoulder to the quiet, tree-shaded street on which she lived. Jefferson Boulevard. The Jeffersons of Jeffersonville lived in the old Jefferson house on Jefferson Boulevard.

It was quite a responsibility.

Sighing, she returned her gaze to his surprisingly sympathetic one. "Since I placed the ad, I've had a few crank calls."

"I'm not a crank," he insisted. "So when do classes start?"

"Classes start when I obtain pupils. Genuine pupils," she emphasized. "Elementary-age pupils. Little boys and little girls whose parents want them to learn to behave graciously but don't have time to teach them. Children to whom dinner is fast food grabbed on the way to someplace or another. Kids who have lost the art of conversation to video games and television."

"Yes! You're right." Kyle's head bobbed up and down, ruining his slicked-down part. "You're absolutely right. And those kids grow up like my...like me."

"The vice president of a successful company," she said dryly.

"No—socially, uh—" he shrugged "—impaired?"

He acted earnest but sounded, to Maggie's ears, a touch patronizing. *Socially impaired.* "What happened? Did you attend a dinner and become confused because there was more than one fork?"

"Actually, there weren't any forks at all."

"How unfortunate."

"No, it was great." He bobbed his head again, irritating Maggie. "Silverware is a source of great anxiety to me."

A warm breeze puffed its way inside, blowing her long hair across her face. Impatiently, she tucked a lock behind her ear. "Just remember, 'outside in.'"

"Huh?"

"Use whatever silverware you have from the outside all the way toward the plate. When you run out, dinner is over. There. Think of all the money and time I've saved you." Maggie gestured toward the open door.

"That's all?"

"I believe so, Mr. McCormick."

"Why?"

"Let's just say you've failed to convince me of your sincerity."

Behind the broken glasses with the taped frame, a pair of clear blue eyes turned to ice. A slightly slack jaw hardened and squared. The stoop-shouldered man in front of her seemed to grow a couple of inches. "Thank you," he said in a voice as frigid as his eyes. "Sorry to have wasted your time. Good day, Miss Jefferson."

He nodded curtly and strode out the door, looking dignified in spite of his appearance. Looking like someone else entirely.

Doubt assailed her immediately. Could she have been wrong about him? Maggie chewed her lip. She had not been nice. In fact, she'd been...rude. Even if he'd been poking fun at her after finding one of her flyers, rudeness never justified rudeness. Guilt smote her.

"Mr.—Mitch?"

He stopped at the railing of her gray-painted porch, but he didn't turn around.

Maggie closed the door quietly behind her and joined him outside. "I thought you were making fun of us. Are you?" Sometimes the direct approach was best.

It was the oddest thing. He seemed to shrink. By the time he turned to face her, all evidence of the attractive self-assurance had vanished. "No, I wasn't making fun of you." His grin showed too many teeth. "Why'd you think that?"

"Well...the way you acted and, uh..." Maggie wasn't certain how to indicate the way he was dressed without unduly insulting him. "You don't *look* the way I pictured a vice president of Stuart Computers."

Mitchell crossed his arms over his chest and dislodged the pocket protector. Straightening it, he asked, "How is the vice president of Stuart Computers supposed to look?"

"Well...older and more distinguished—" Maggie broke off. "And not someone who needs etiquette lessons."

He flattened his hair, which kept springing up as if it wanted to part on the opposite side. "If you don't believe me, you don't believe me."

"Sorry," Maggie apologized, not feeling very sorry.

He shrugged. "I malfunction in social situations, so I avoid them," he explained. "But lately I've had to go to some meetings and dinners and stuff for my job, and things haven't gone too well." He took another step nearer. "I thought maybe you could help me?"

He accompanied his plea with a wistful expression that tugged at Maggie's heart.

"Please."

Maggie caught her breath. His voice had deepened from a juvenile tenor to a manly bass. He wasn't smiling right now. He looked older and more mature. It was almost as if she were glimpsing the self-assured man he could become—with her help.

It was a tantalizing glimpse.

"All right," she said and held out her hand, expecting him to shake it.

His gaze never leaving hers, he grasped her hand with both of his, carried it to his lips and kissed it.

"Thank you."

"Goodness!" Maggie laughed and pulled her hand away, her heart fluttering oddly. "Hand kissing hasn't been in favor for a while."

"Pity."

It *was* a pity, Maggie thought, still overly aware of his touch.

Mitch's lips curved with gentle amusement that unsettled Maggie.

"Would...would you care to sit down?" She gestured to the white wooden swing rather than asking him back into the house. For reasons she didn't care to explore, Maggie didn't want her family to overhear her conversation with this man.

"A porch swing! I haven't sat in one of these for a long time." Without waiting for her to sit first, Mitch plopped himself in the swing. When Maggie gingerly joined him, he threw an arm across the back, withdrawing it hurriedly when she flinched forward.

Until she'd moved to Atlanta, there hadn't been men in Maggie's life, and she didn't trust them. She'd never known her grandfather or her father and Opal's traveling salesman didn't count. If it hadn't been for her cousin Coral, Maggie might have wondered if there really *had* been a salesman, traveling or otherwise.

Maggie had dated while she was in school, but only rarely. Bringing home a date meant he was subjected to a grand inquisition led by her grandmother. Her mother would sit quietly by, interjecting feminist dogma to see what sort of reaction she got. Opal, after ascertaining that Maggie's date neither knew nor was related to anyone who had appeared on stage, screen or television, would drift away on an air of disappointment.

On the whole, Maggie didn't think much of men, and her experience with the blue-eyed Brady Babcock she'd thought was "the one" hadn't changed her opinion.

Oh, well, that was a lifetime ago and she had other pressing problems, like getting pupils for the charm school.

She hadn't considered teaching adults, but then, she thought as Mitchell set the swing rocking, perhaps he wasn't so different from elementary-age boys, after all.

Accompanied by the familiar comforting creak of the wooden swing, Maggie cleared her throat. "You mentioned that a difficult experience in a business situation brought you to us?"

"Huh?" Mitch turned his head to look at her, causing his glasses to slide down his nose. He pushed them back into place.

"You decided to enroll in charm school for a reason. Might I know that reason?" she probed.

Mitch squirmed and kicked the swing higher. "Why?"

"As I told you, I intended to teach children," Maggie explained, becoming more relaxed the more childishly he behaved. "I planned to begin with very basic manners and progress to advanced social behavior."

"Sounds good."

He was absolutely no help. "I assume you wished to brush up on business etiquette?"

Mitch sat against the back of the swing and dragged his feet. "Before we start anything, I suppose I ought to admit I think this etiquette stuff is a waste of time. If people are offended by what fork you use, then that's their problem."

"Etiquette isn't only about silverware. It's just an awareness of society's customs in dealing with people." Although he didn't know it, Maggie was quoting from her own introductory speech.

"I think there are more important things to worry about than a bunch of silly rules," he grumbled.

"If you think that, then why are you here?"

The swing slowed. "Let's say that I was strongly encouraged to come."

Maggie spread her hands in bafflement. "If you don't want to learn, I can't teach you anything."

Mitch leaned forward and propped his elbows on his knees. "Are you saying there's no hope for a guy like me?"

The afternoon breeze ruffled his hair. He'd apparently applied some dark goo to hold it down and the whole thing lifted to reveal a lighter brown underneath.

Maggie wondered if she should work personal grooming into her lessons. "If you want to learn, I can teach you. However, I do not intend to justify the subject I teach."

He groaned. "I'll never remember all those silly little rules and things. You don't suppose there's an etiquette software program?"

Maggie laughed, in spite of herself. "Probably, but I'm not going to use it—and you're not, either."

His face fell and she laughed again.

"You can't consult your computer every time you're having an etiquette crisis."

"But I could. You see, I've got a laptop—"

Maggie shuddered. "You'll just have to memorize all the rules until they become second nature."

"But I *can't!* I get so caught up with my work that...well, I..." Mitch stopped, wearing a resentful expression. "I've been told that I've acted insulting." He looked earnestly at her. "I didn't do it on purpose!"

"I'm sure you didn't," Maggie said soothingly. "And you'd like to learn how to avoid insulting people again, right?"

Mitch's gaze slid away. "Right. So what do you think? Can you teach an adult to..." He gestured mutely.

"Act like an adult?" Maggie supplied. "I'm willing to try if you are." She thought for a moment. "Give me a few days to prepare lessons—"

"No!" Mitch interrupted. "I want to start now. The whole thing. From the beginning. Start from scratch and work up to business etiquette. Know anything about Japanese customs?"

Baffled, Maggie shook her head.

"Well, look them up." Mitch slapped his hands against his knees and stood, jouncing Maggie in the swing. "I'm going to be working with the Japanese. Concentrate particularly on those customs that differ from ours. Zero in and emphasize the ones that cause offense. Have the syllabus ready for me to review at our next meeting."

Maggie blinked. Was this man giving orders—this attractive man—the same one who'd pleaded for help moments ago?

She said nothing. He glanced down at her and appeared to catch himself. "Uh, that is, if you think my suggestions are appropriate."

Maggie nodded, thoroughly confused. He was acting like two different men.

"When do you want to start?" Visibly impatient, he glanced at his watch, a huge plastic gadget with digital readout.

He hadn't asked about tuition, which was good since she hadn't considered what to charge for a private pupil. "Do you want to meet on Tuesday and Thursday, or Monday, Wednesday and Friday?"

"Oh, three times a week. We've got a lot of work ahead of us. See you tomorrow, then? Say, four o'clock?"

"I—okay."

Mitch barely waited for her nod before lifting a hand in farewell and jogging down the front steps.

Still trying to figure out exactly who and what Mitchell McCormick was, Maggie followed his progress, her eyes widening when he stopped at a sporty little red car, blipped the alarm and hopped inside. He tossed the broken glasses on the seat beside him and started the car, gunning the engine.

Then, with tires squealing, Maggie's first pupil smoked down Jefferson Boulevard.

THAT WENT WELL, Kyle thought, except he was going to cut it close for his next appointment. He wanted to change out of Mitch's clothes before his dinner meeting with Harlan Edwards of Drake Office Supply. He'd just bought three expensive photocopiers from Drake and now hoped to sell Edwards on a new computer system. He'd heard that Drake was considering upgrading the computers in their regional offices and since Stuart Computers had just bought the photocopiers, Drake ought to listen to a sales pitch.

Kyle planned to attend the dinner alone. He wanted no chance of repeating the fiasco he'd encountered with the Japanese.

His skin crawled when he thought of the potential business lost due to the bungling of his friends and business partners.

Four of them, Kyle, Mitch, Pat and Lane had started Stuart Computers when they were still in school. Kyle was the drive and primary source of funds. The others were happy to stay in the background and become quietly wealthy. The system had worked fine for years. Now it didn't.

But if he got the rights to use the memory chip, which he would if Miss My-Ancestor-Founded-The-Town came through, all would work again.

Maggie Jefferson was a pleasant surprise. More than pleasant. She was young and didn't act like a relic from the last century. And she was pretty, in a conservative, traditional way. Softer. Leggier. And the way he'd caught her studying him made him forget he was supposed to be acting like Mitch.

She'd been kind, but firm with him. Just what Mitch needed. If their next meeting went well and Kyle liked her plans for the course, he couldn't see any reason not to hire her. Any woman who could thrive in the fossilized atmosphere of that house could handle Mitch and the others. Kyle hadn't worked out how to tell her he wasn't Mitchell McCormick, but he'd worry about that later.

All in all, he was rather pleased with himself as he parked his car and unlocked the side door of the Stuart building. He would prefer that no one see him dressed like this—especially Mitch, who didn't know Kyle had borrowed his clothes.

The building boasted a dormitory wing with a fully stocked kitchen to accommodate those computer wizards who lost track of time or had middle-of-the-night flashes of brilliance. This college-like atmosphere and Kyle's laid-back management system was the reason that Stuart Computers was the most sought-after employer in the South.

Lately, though, and especially with increased business socializing, Kyle felt as if he'd aged while his cofounders hadn't. He'd caught himself sternly reminding them to complete projects when their experimentation zoomed off on a tangent.

To them, Stuart Computers was still fun. But as the company expanded, Kyle felt the stress of being responsible for the livelihood of hundreds of employees and their families.

This afternoon, pretending to be Mitch was fun, Kyle realized as he entered the dormitory and furtively changed out of his friend's clothes, washed out the dark hairdressing and put on one of his own tailored suits. The first fun he'd had in a long time.

Slipping out of the dormitory, he jogged up all four flights of stairs at the back of the building and reached his office undetected.

He gathered the files on Drake before noticing a pink message slip taped to his telephone. Harlan Edwards had been delayed about thirty minutes.

Breathing a sigh of relief, Kyle collapsed on his smooth leather couch to take a breather.

He intended to use the time reviewing the Drake files, but found himself thinking of Maggie Jefferson instead.

He'd heard people described as having "hidden depths," and now that he'd met Maggie, he knew what the words meant. In fact, it was almost as though someone else was hiding beneath the determinedly ladylike exterior she'd worn. She wasn't the sort of person he'd expect to run a charm school. That would be more the expertise of the older women whose tea he'd disrupted.

Tripping over the tea table had been unintentional, but may have swayed Maggie to accept him as a pupil. He winced as he remembered the horrified expressions on the Jefferson women's faces and the incredulous look on Maggie's as he lay at her feet. Nice set of legs on that girl...

He should apologize. He grabbed the phone on the side table and punched the intercom. "Janet, are you still here?"

"I'm just fixin' to leave," his secretary answered.

"Would you—" Kyle was about to ask her to send flowers to the Jefferson women. But that was a gracious gesture, something that wouldn't occur to Mitch. "Would you come in here, please?" he amended, feeling guilty at his decision to forgo the flowers. All for a good cause, he rationalized. If he did hire Maggie, she'd be well compensated.

"Oh, good, you got my message," Janet said on her way in. "I was afraid you wouldn't stop by here first."

"I wanted these with me." He tapped the files, then closed them. "Have you got a minute to talk?"

"Just one," she said, holding up a finger. "The boys have basketball practice after school and they'll be starved for dinner."

"Call out for pizza—my treat," Kyle offered, remembering his own voracious teenage appetite.

"Okay!" Janet cheerfully sat on the sofa opposite him. A plump woman in her forties, his secretary was the company's oldest employee, a statistic she was reminded of yearly. Each birthday, Kyle presented her with a huge cake adorned with the appropriate number of candles, then gave her the rest of the day off.

"You grew up in Jeffersonville, didn't you?" he asked.

"Yes and never thought I'd still be living here," she confirmed.

"Tell me what you know about the Jefferson family." Kyle stood and walked to the small, wood-paneled refrigerator built into the bar.

"You mean you're finally aiming to stand up to the Jefferson Jewels?"

"Is that what they're called?" Ignoring her question, he reached inside the refrigerator and pulled out a cherry cola, Janet's secret weakness. He gestured with the can and raised his eyebrows.

Nodding, Janet settled back into the couch. "Pearl and her sister, Opal, live in the old Jefferson house— it's been designated as an official historic landmark, you know."

Kyle nodded, filing away the information.

"Well, they live there with Pearl's daughter, Ruby. Opal's daughter, Coral, works in the Savannah Home for Unwed Mothers—a place where she can put all that family experience to good use," Janet muttered.

"What experience?" Kyle asked.

Giving him a significant look, she said, "It's not for me to be telling tales out of school."

Smiling to himself, Kyle asked, "What about Maggie?"

"Oh, have you met her?" Janet's eyes immediately

gleamed with a matchmaking light Kyle had seen before. "She's Ruby's daughter—and just a few years younger than you. I heard she'd been working in Atlanta for some fancy corporation and got laid off. She's been back here a couple of months now. That girl's got a rebellious streak in her, just like Ruby, but she can hide hers better." Janet gave him a speculative look. "You like girls with a little bit of spice in them, don't you?"

More and more, Kyle thought. He handed Janet the glass of cola, quickly asking another question before her speculating got out of control. "What about the Jefferson men?"

"Maggie's not married, that I know of."

"The rest of the men," he prompted dryly. Kyle knew he'd never convince Janet that Maggie hadn't caught his eye—especially since she had—but gossip now would ruin everything.

"Well..." Janet sipped her drink. "You can hardly miss that statue of LaRue Jefferson in the center of town. It seems like every street meanders past—"

"Any *living* Jefferson men?" Kyle interrupted, rubbing his forehead. His secretary was full of information, though at times it was difficult to access. This was proving to be one of those times.

"Hard to say." Janet drained her glass, stood and carried it to the bar. "Pearl's husband—that would be Maggie's grandfather," she explained. "He never came back from the war."

"Which war?"

"Two." Janet eyed the refrigerator, forgoing a second drink with obvious reluctance. "I think they got married—or so Pearl says—on a Saturday and he shipped out Monday. Opal ran off with a traveling salesman, then came back without him, and Ruby..." Janet threw back her head and sighed, staring at the ceiling. "I was in school with Ruby. We went off to different colleges, though. I saw her one Christmas break. By the time I came home that summer, little Maggie was on the way." Janet gave Kyle a significant look, allowing him to draw his own conclusions.

"Now, there was talk of a soldier husband who went off to Vietnam, but *I* never saw a wedding announcement. 'Course, Pearl stared down anyone who put around that Ruby had jumped the traces before she'd jumped the broom. And Ruby stayed pretty close-mouthed about the whole thing."

"Jumped the broom?"

"Got married." Janet seemed to recollect her match-making hopes. "But they're Jeffersonville's first family and they still call the shots in this town."

"Don't I know it," Kyle said with feeling. "They'd love it if I left town."

"Now I know you and Pearl got crosswise, but you hang in there and remember that the sun don't shine on the same dog's tail all the time."

3

"I'M NOT ENTIRELY CERTAIN it is proper for Magnolia to tutor that young man unchaperoned." Pearl peered over her half glasses at the others, waiting for their automatic agreement.

Silence. Ruby looked up from a dog-eared paper, glanced at her mother, then at Maggie, then back to the paper. Opal raised her eyebrows and bit her lip.

Maggie reminded herself that now was not the time to point out that until recently, she'd been living unchaperoned in Atlanta. "I do think Mr. McCormick will be more comfortable without an audience."

Everyone was gathered in the dining room. Pearl and Opal were planning a pink tea in honor of the granddaughter of a dear friend and they made Ruby take part whether she wanted to or not.

It was Friday afternoon, and Maggie had just asked to be excused. It wasn't as though any real planning was necessary for the tea. The menu would be the same as it had been a hundred times before: tiny chicken-salad sandwiches with the crusts cut off, pink petits fours, pink butter mints and rolled lace cookies filled with cherry whipped cream.

"Opal, would you check the icebox and see if we're out of mayonnaise?" Pearl asked sweetly.

"I will, but only if you promise that you won't add your lace cookies to the menu. The cream runs by the end of the party and it makes the plate look so tacky." Opal's forehead wrinkled in distress, until she realized she was frowning and gently massaged the wrinkles away.

Maggie smiled to herself. They were never out of mayonnaise and Pearl would always insist on serving the lace cookies.

"If a young woman can eat a lace cookie with elegance, then her debut will be a success," Pearl stated, adding lace cookies to the list of party food. "And no matter how precious Martha Jane's granddaughter is, if Rebecca Ann can't eat one of my lace cookies, then it will be a waste of time to sponsor her."

With a genteel stamp of her foot, Opal left to check the icebox.

"Grandmother, Mr. McCormick will be here any moment—"

"Just a minute, Magnolia." Her grandmother turned to Ruby, who was quietly and industriously addressing envelopes. "I believe we've yet to decide on the guest list, Ruby."

Maggie's mother mumbled.

"Those aren't the Crane envelopes—Ruby!"

Maggie's mother flinched, but kept writing. "I want these to go out in today's mail. They're announcements for the rally we're having to protest the cut in funds to the women's shelter in Augusta." Ruby gazed at her mother. "You ought to come, too."

Maggie picked up a bunch of the envelopes. "Mama,

several of these are in-town addresses. If you'd phone, you'd save on postage."

Ruby snatched back her envelopes. "If we're so desperate we can't spare a few dollars to help womankind, then we have no business giving a tea—pink or otherwise."

"Not give the tea?" Opal had returned. "But Rebecca Ann—"

"Of course we're giving the tea. It's our duty." Pearl reached for the box of index cards on which she'd written the addresses of everyone who was anyone in Jeffersonville, and Atlanta, too, for that matter.

Maggie took one look at her mother's face and began discreetly moving toward the door. "Duty?" she heard Ruby begin dangerously. "Don't you think we have a duty to support a place of refuge for women who have nowhere to go?"

"I think we have a duty to help those we can," Pearl replied, her voice still calm, but gaining in volume. Maggie edged nearer the door. Opal's mouth was an "O" of distress, but Maggie saw her hand creeping toward the food list and knew she was going to use the incipient argument as a distraction during which she could cross lace cookies off the menu.

"And how does throwing a pink tea for Martha's granddaughter help all womankind?"

Taking a deep breath, Maggie slipped out the door, but stayed nearby to hear Pearl's rejoinder.

"We must do all we can to secure Rebecca Ann's successful debut. It will chart the course for the rest of her life."

"You mean so she can snag a rich husband!"

Maggie winced and walked quickly to the foyer. Soft southern drawls that weren't so soft anymore followed her.

Peering through the lace curtains, she saw a mist of red. That would be Mitch's car. The arguing was clearly audible, so Maggie stepped out onto the front porch.

It was Mitch's red car, all right, but he wasn't driving it. The driver expertly maneuvered the sports car next to the curb on Maggie's tree-lined street. He parked quickly, with no jostling back and forth. Of course, the sleek little car would be easier to park than an ancient Cadillac, Maggie thought, wistfully remembering her own sporty model.

The man jumped from the car and strode up the front walk, checking his watch before noticing her.

He faltered immediately, then continued walking, a wary expression on his face.

Maggie could only stare and wish she'd checked her appearance in the hall mirror before stepping outside. The man was gorgeous. Definitely not a Jeffersonville native.

He bounded up the steps. "Hello, Maggie."

The voice was familiar. And the eyes—blue. Pure blue. True blue, American blue, Georgia-sky-in-August blue.

Mitchell McCormick blue. It couldn't be. "Mr. McCormick?"

"Not exactly."

A Maggie-dreaming-about-them-when-she-should-be-paying-attention blue. She gave herself a mental shake. "I don't understand."

"It's complicated."

In twenty-four hours he'd turned from a frog into a prince. She *bet* it was complicated. "So give it your best shot."

He glanced over her shoulder to the open window.

Maggie caught the words *food coloring* and knew Opal and Pearl were arguing over how deep a pink to tint the icing on the petits fours. Pearl would want the icing to match the cake—sign of attention to detail—and Opal liked the contrast of two pinks. Ruby was silent. She'd once dyed the cake batter green, but Pearl had discovered it in time to substitute store-bought. She'd been compensating for the shame ever since.

"I am the man you met yesterday—in a way—but I'm not Mitchell McCormick. I only pretended to be."

Maggie stepped back. "Then this *is* a joke, right?" Disappointment shot through her. Once again, she'd been betrayed by a pair of blue eyes. "I knew nobody could be so...socially clueless."

"Oh, Mitch is, believe me."

"Why should I? I don't even know who you really are."

The man hesitated. "I'm Mitch's friend."

After a waffling answer like that, Maggie should march right back into the house and slam the door. But...she couldn't. There was something about handsome men—and this one in particular—that made women allow them more leeway than was perhaps wise. And the women in Maggie's family had allowed men *lots* of leeway. "Some friend you are."

He smiled, his eyes crinkling at the corners, settling into a pattern of lines and creases with an ease that told her he smiled often. "My portrayal of Mitch in a social situation yesterday was, unfortunately, uncannily accurate. He needs your help."

"So why isn't he here?"

Mitch's friend gestured to the porch swing. "Could we...?"

Maggie eyed him. She still didn't know who he was, but they were on her front porch with an open window behind them. This was as safe as it could get in Jeffersonville. Nodding curtly, she sat, intending to remain as far from him as possible, yet finding herself inching closer to the middle.

The man turned his incredible blue eyes on her.

Her mouth went dry. Maggie hoped the explanation was a lengthy one.

She'd never thought of herself as a superficial person, solely influenced by someone's appearance. But...he looked so *different* than he had yesterday. He even looked taller, but maybe that was because his hair wasn't squashed down with that dark gunk. He'd parted it on the other side, too, and sun-bleached strands of expertly cut hair now gleamed in the afternoon light.

His transformation caused her to be so much more *aware* of him. She was appalled that her baser instincts were so easily swayed. But she figured that's why they were called "baser" instincts.

"Mitch is very resistant to any sort of social coaching," he told her. "He's a brilliant man, but as with so many brilliant people, there are areas which are correspondingly..." He gestured as he searched for words.

"Not brilliant," Maggie supplied.

"Yes." He smiled, showing teeth impossibly white and even. "The thing of it is, Mitch's lack of polish is becoming a liability to him in business situations. I saw your advertisement and suggested he give you a call. He refused, so I decided to check you out, myself."

"And did we check out?" she asked.

"Yes, I think so," he answered, missing the sarcasm. "I still need to see the course syllabus, though."

"And if that meets your satisfaction, then what? Will you hog-tie Mr. McCormick to get him here?"

He glanced at her. "I'd hoped to persuade you to go to him."

Blue eyes, or not, this man had used up all his leeway. "I don't even know your name."

"I'm aware of that. It's...a separate issue."

What? "If you don't want me to tell your friend who contacted me, I won't, but if I don't see some ID right now, our conversation is over." Maggie stood.

He stood, as well. "First tell me if you'd be at all interested in conducting business-etiquette seminars to a whole roomful of Mitches."

"A whole roomful?" Her mind boggled. However, this man had said the key words *business* and *seminars*. That meant a corporate account, which meant serious money, and Maggie needed serious money. "You realize that would be costly."

"How costly?"

Maggie shook her head. "I'm not going to be tricked into giving you a price before I study what's involved. Now, who are you?"

He blinked once. "Kyle Stuart."

Oh, right. "I don't like jokes. My fee just doubled."

His expression didn't change. "I'll pay it."

Maggie stared at him. He stared back. "Are you *really* Kyle Stuart, the Stuart Computers Kyle Stuart?"

He nodded, watching her.

"Are you *crazy?*" The last word ended with an uncharming screech. "What are you *doing* here?"

"Shh. Keep your voice down."

They both looked toward the window.

"Raspberry will make the punch take on an unattractive blue tone," they heard Pearl say. "And you'll never get all the seeds out."

"Your strawberry-cloud punch is becoming dated, and it's so sticky. Wouldn't a nice tart raspberry lemonade be ever so much nicer?" Opal wheedled.

"But the word *tart* has such unlovely connotations."

"Mama, knowing Rebecca Ann, it's entirely appropriate."

"Ruby!"

KYLE CAUGHT MAGGIE hiding a smile and felt his heart rate accelerate. "I assume that the fact that you have neither screamed nor thrown me off your porch means you're willing to listen?"

She eyed him, then gracefully reclaimed her seat on

the porch swing. "Why scream? They wouldn't hear me."

Kyle sat down, relief coursing through him. He was by no means safe, but at least he was still in the game.

Maggie tilted her head. "On the other hand, after I figure out why you're here, I might still scream and throw you off the porch."

Kyle held up his hands, palms outward. "Etiquette seminars, I swear. Mitch and the others—they act like they're still in college. They're offending potential clients and losing business."

She turned in the swing and propped her chin on her knuckles, looking as though she was settling in for a long talk. "Why me? I mean, I realize personnel training is my field, but I haven't taught business etiquette before."

"You're a corporate trainer?" The gods were smiling.

"Yes, I conducted courses in personnel training for Hinds in Atlanta before they decided to outsource their management program."

His secretary had mentioned that Maggie had been living in Atlanta. "That's great." Fabulous. Lucky beyond his wildest dreams. The chip was as good as his.

"You didn't know?" Suspicion clouded her voice.

He hadn't seen the trap until too late. Reluctantly, he shook his head.

Her eyes narrowed. "You're my grandmother's mortal enemy—and I don't think that's overstating it— *why* would you want anything to do with us, when I know there are companies who specialize in this very thing?" There wasn't very much of the soft Maggie in her expression now.

"I am *not* your grandmother's mortal enemy. The Civil War ended over a hundred years ago. You people have got to move on."

"How can we when you plunked down your stupid glass skyscraper on our park!"

"What park? I bought a piece of abandoned property."

"Yes, the Holcombe place. It was always understood that after Mr. Holcombe passed on to his reward, the land would become Jefferson Park."

"Someone should have told the Holcombes. They're the ones who sold it to me."

"Only after you waved a fistful of Yankee dollars in their faces!"

"If your grandmother wanted the land so much, why didn't *she* buy it? It had been for sale long enough."

Maggie's face closed and her lips tightened. "Grandmother felt that it should become city property."

In other words, the old gal wasn't willing to pony up the cash. Hardheaded *and* tightfisted. "I guess the city didn't agree, because they were sure eager to welcome my company and the jobs it brought to Jeffersonville."

"Even so, you didn't have to rub her nose in your victory by naming the park after yourself."

Kyle stared. So that was it. The park. He should have figured it out for himself. "That wasn't my idea, but I kind of liked it. No one in my family has ever had a park named after him."

"Nor in my family—that's the point."

"Give me a break. There's Jefferson junk all over this town!"

Incredibly, Maggie laughed. "I know. Imagine *being* a Jefferson."

"It would certainly make life a lot easier."

"That's what you think." Maggie gazed out over the porch railing.

"Ruby Jefferson, the tea will be next Sunday afternoon and I'll expect you to be there!" Pearl's voice sounded clearly.

Maggie winced. "Mama must have a prior engagement that conflicts with the pink tea."

"What is a pink tea?" If it was some secret southern custom, Kyle wanted to know about it. The Japanese liked tea, maybe they'd like one of these.

"It's just a tea party, but all the food and decorations are pink and people dress in pink."

"Oh." Women stuff.

"It's how we introduce new women to the community—say, the fiancée of someone's son, or a girl who's about to make her debut."

"So you have to put the Jefferson seal of approval on everybody, right?"

Maggie's eyes turned glacial. "Not *everyone* merits the Jefferson seal of approval."

Kyle knew he was distinctly unapproved. "Look." He turned in the swing, mimicking her body language. It was a trick he'd learned from his sales experience. "If I rename the park for your great-great-whatever, will that make things right with your grandmother?"

She shook her head. "You don't get it, do you? It's not just the park, it's how you came into town and turned up your nose at the way we did things. Did you try to fit in? No. You wanted an office building and by golly, you built one, without any thought to the way it fit in with the rest of the town. And then you brought in all these new people who ignored everybody who didn't work for your company. Not one person—including you, *especially you*—ever called on my grandmother."

"I called her!"

"Called *on* her. There's a difference." One that had obviously escaped him, her look said. "You spoke with the chamber of commerce, you met with the mayor, you even talked with the school-board president, yet you didn't bother to acknowledge the existence of...of—" Maggie broke off with a frustrated grimace. "Oh, I'll just say it—of the woman who's been the head of Jeffersonville society for over fifty years!"

During her diatribe, Kyle felt his jaw go slack. *He'd had the same small-town problems as that unfortunate Japanese firm Matsuzaka had told him about. And he hadn't even known it.* Stunned, he groped for something to say, something that could salvage a situation that was far worse than he'd known.

"You didn't have a clue, did you?"

"No," he admitted, thinking he'd been acting too superior around Mitch.

"I didn't think so. And if I thought you'd deliberately insulted my grandmother, then we wouldn't still be having this conversation."

Kyle didn't doubt her for an instant. "Is there anything I can— Wait." He grinned. "The pavilion."

"What pavilion?"

"For the park. We're building an old-fashioned outdoor bandstand. We'll name it Jefferson Pavilion. How about that?"

Maggie nodded slowly. "Might work. Which brings us back to why? Why do you care about being nice to my grandmother all of a sudden?"

Kyle didn't know whether to confide in Maggie or not. Just when he thought he had her figured as a Jefferson rogue, she lit into him about her grandmother. Once he told her about the Japanese and their emphasis on a receptive community, Maggie Jefferson would have far too much power over his company's future. One demonstration organized by that mother of hers, and the Japanese would flee.

"It's either got to have something to do with your company or with a woman," Maggie mused aloud.

"A woman?"

She set the swing in motion. "Yes. If you were involved with a woman and she wanted to have any kind of social life here, she'd want you to patch things up with my grandmother."

Kyle wanted to point out that his being in disgrace with her grandmother hadn't bothered any number of women in Jeffersonville, but didn't. "I'm not currently seeing anyone."

"Then it's got to be your company." She pressed the knuckle of her index finger to her mouth. "Now, what could we have that you want?" She spoke softly, as though to herself.

Kyle couldn't stand it anymore. He was a risk taker and now was the time to go for it. "In June, a Japanese company will be coming to tour the plant *and* Jeffersonville. They've developed a new memory chip that I want to use in my computers. If that happens, it will mean that they'll move some of their people to Jeffersonville." He smiled tightly. "And since they're much smarter than I am, they're checking out the community first, because they want to make sure they're welcome here."

"And if they don't like Jeffersonville?"

"They'll go with another company." He looked her right in her big brown eyes, letting her see his confidence and strength. It was the same look he gave clients, investors and tax auditors. Part bluff, part charm, it was the patented Kyle Stuart Look that had served him just fine, thank you very much.

"Mr. Stuart, all the color has left your face."

He shouldn't have tried to give her the Look. Too much was at stake. "Good thing I'm not a poker player."

"It's a good thing I am."

Kyle gave a surprised laugh before groaning. "This is not my day."

"This...chip...?" At his nod, she continued. "Is this chip that important?"

"Yes." If he could only make her understand. "They've used submicron X-ray lithography to de-

velop a super-high-density, ultra-low-power fast
memory chip." He gestured. "It's *ten* gigabits."

Maggie held up her hand. "I'll concede the chip's
importance."

"Sorry, I get carried away. It's just that it's the next
generation. The computer that offers it will set the new
standard." He spread his hands. "I want it to be in a
Stuart computer."

"Why don't the Japanese use their own computers?"

"Import taxes and the fact that I've already got the
manufacturing facilities and the distribution in place.
They know that by the time they'd cut through all the
red tape in this country, someone else could have developed a similar chip."

She was concentrating on what he was telling her.
Encouraged, Kyle reached across the wooded slats and
grasped her hands. She looked surprised, but he didn't
care. "I want you to know what's at stake here. Though
we've been in a slump, I haven't laid off a single person. If we don't get this chip, the value of our computers will sink. Then I'll have to cut back on staff. I might
even have to sell the building. So, yes, you Jeffersons
could run me out of town. But if I leave, all the jobs
leave with me. And if you think my building is ugly
now, picture it after it's stood vacant a few years, because I guarantee no other company will buy it after
they hear what happened to me."

"Kyle—my hands."

He was squeezing them. Releasing his grip, he
rubbed her fingers. "I'm sorry." He looked into her

wide brown eyes. "Well, there you have it. Ball's in your court."

She smiled faintly. "Why do men always use sports analogies?"

"I—"

They both jumped at the movement behind them. "I'll just open this window a skosh more to catch a cross breeze. Magnolia, you and Mr. McCormick have been out here for quite—"

Through the screen, Kyle saw Pearl Jefferson's face freeze in horror. "You!"

4

"MAGNOLIA, YOU COME into the house right this instant!"

"Grandmother—"

"This *instant!*" Pearl headed for the front door.

Maggie had to make a decision at once. Kyle, his lips tight, stared at her. Her hands still tingled where he'd gripped them as he'd explained how important this super-duper computer chip was.

Her grandmother would never listen to him, but Maggie wasn't her grandmother. And she *had* listened to him. What's more, she saw his point.

But would she be so open-minded if he weren't the best-looking man she'd seen since returning to Jeffersonville?

Choosing not to examine her motives too closely, she whispered, "Eight-thirty at the old Garthwhiddle place," and leaped out of the swing just before Pearl marched onto the porch.

"Magnolia Blossom Jefferson, I told you to come inside. Do you know who this man is?"

Maggie gazed steadily at Pearl. "Yes, Grandmother."

Pearl's head reared back. "I'll speak with you later, young lady." There was an ominous tone in her voice.

She was also brandishing a broom. "Get off my porch, you Yankee!"

Kyle inclined his head. "Good day, Mrs. Jefferson." His tone was scrupulously polite as he attempted an elegant exit. Maggie gave him points for style.

Pearl nudged him along with her broom.

"Grandmother, really!" Maggie admonished from the doorway.

Her grandmother whipped around and nudged her, too.

"Ow!"

"Inside!"

Muttering to herself, Maggie stalked into the house, knowing now was not the time to make a stand. But she was a grown woman. She'd donned the sweetly behaved Jefferson image out of deference to her grandmother, but she resented being treated like a fifteen-year-old who'd been caught kissing the gardener's son.

Not that Maggie ever had. Been caught, that is.

"What's going on, Maggie?" Her mother and Opal had come to the foyer. Opal had positioned her hands over her heart, her favorite pose for hearing unpleasant news.

"Grandmother has just discovered that I was talking to Kyle Stuart on the front porch. I believe she's running him off with a broom."

"Good gracious, Lord a'mighty." Opal slapped both hands against her cheeks and hurried to look.

"What did he want?" Ruby asked.

Maggie hesitated. She'd never been very good at predicting her mother's reactions to anything. "He was inquiring about business-etiquette courses for his employees."

"Sounds harmless."

"I thought so. In fact—" Maggie decided to send out a little preliminary tester "—he doesn't seem to be quite the ogre Grandmother said he was."

Maggie's mother had been reknotting the crocheted shawl she wore, but at Maggie's words, she looked up. "And how did he seem?"

The way her mother stared at her unsettled Maggie. The hate the Jewels felt for Kyle Stuart must run very deep. "He seemed...reasonable. For what it's worth, I don't believe he intended to insult Grandmother."

Ruby continued to gaze at her. Stepping forward, she pushed Maggie's hair away from her face and tilted her chin from side to side.

"What?" Maggie asked, feeling her face heat as though her mother could sense Maggie's intended rendezvous with the enemy.

"Be careful, Maggie," was all Ruby said before walking back into the dining room.

The screen door banged. "Magnolia!"

Maggie had hoped to escape to her room.

"How dare you consort with that man?"

"Now, Pearl, don't overset yourself." Opal, wearing her three-inch heels, struggled to keep up with her sister. "You don't want to have a heart attack the way Dane Rockwell on 'Sinners and Saviors' did after his daughter, Letitia, married his former business partner so he could get control of the stock."

"Opal?"

"Yes, Pearl?"

"The invitations?"

"Oh! Yes, of course." Opal started to mince her way to the dining room, then called back to them. "Now don't worry about Letitia. She discovered the treachery during Dane's funeral."

"Good for her," Maggie said. "Grandmother, do you need help with the invitations?"

Pearl was not to be diverted. "Magnolia, why did you not alert me to Mr. Stuart's presence?"

"I didn't know who he was until midway through our conversation."

"Am I to understand that you are in the habit of conversing with any strange man who happens by?"

"Only the cute ones."

Pearl's nostrils flared. "You are being impertinent. Go to your room."

That worked out nicely. Although, Maggie thought, things had pretty much hit rock bottom when a twenty-eight-year-old was sent to her room.

She refrained from slamming the door, instead flinging herself onto the too-soft mattress covered with the feminist quilt her mother had sewn for her. While other babies might have had nursery rhymes, Maggie had grown up wrapped in embroidered quotes about equal rights.

Yet here she was, banished to her room, unemployed and dressed as though she'd been to a garden party. Life wasn't working out quite the way she'd planned.

She wondered if her mother was disappointed in

her. Ruby had tried to leave the smothering life-style in Jeffersonville, and then had been forced to return when she was pregnant with Maggie. Maggie had always felt she owed it to her mother to take advantage of some of those equal rights Ruby continued to fight for.

Now Maggie was back, and it looked as if she was staying awhile.

Standing suddenly, she unzipped her skirt and kicked it across the room, then unearthed the jeans she'd buried in the bottom of the bureau.

Once she felt more like herself—or the self she was when she wasn't living with her grandmother—Maggie thought about the situation with Kyle.

After six years of hearing how the Stuart Computers people were destroying Jeffersonville, it took some mental adjusting for Maggie to think of Kyle as an ally.

Not, she was ashamed to acknowledge, a whole lot of adjusting. There'd been something appealing about him even when he was in his Mitchell guise, and now that she'd seen the real man...how had he managed to escape Jeffersonville's matchmaking mamas for the past six years?

In spite of what he'd said, she knew that some would snub him because Pearl had decreed that he must be snubbed, but those who had never achieved the "Jefferson stamp of approval," as he'd called it, would have been after him with a vengeance.

In fact... Maggie grabbed her pillow and stared at the ceiling. It would be difficult to be around him and not succumb to his charm. Those eyes of his could be her downfall, not that she'd ever let him know it.

There was a knock on her door.

"Come in," Maggie called, suspecting it was her mother.

Sure enough, Ruby carried a tray into her room. "Maggie..."

Maggie laughed. "Don't worry, Mama, I know the drill. I'm to eat my supper in my room and ponder my behavior."

Ruby laughed, a rarity. "I can't believe I'm back to bringing you supper trays after all these years."

"Well, I sassed her. I deserve it."

"You just don't want to have to listen to her at the dinner table."

Maggie grinned. "Sorry about that."

Ruby waved away her apology. "It's good for her. She's been stewing all these years. Now she's had a chance to let off some steam and tell Mr. Stuart what she thinks of him to his face."

"Or his back," Maggie murmured as her mother closed the door.

Thinking of the three women who'd raised her brought a sudden stinging of tears to her eyes. She loved them and their ways, even if she didn't always agree. How would they cope if they lost the house? How was she going to support the three of them, plus herself?

And they didn't even know they were in trouble.

Money, where it came from, how one acquired it or what one used it for was never discussed when Maggie was growing up. Money was just always there. She shuddered to think of what would have happened to them if she hadn't begun investigating the family finances.

It had all started with that pesky leak. After she lost her job, she'd sought to occupy her enforced idleness by overseeing some cosmetic refurbishing. The ceiling leak had stained the wallpaper in the second-best upstairs bedroom. It was easy to forget about the stain because the room was rarely used, but since Maggie had time on her hands, she'd decided to see if anywhere else in the house could benefit from a coat of paint or new wallpaper.

Unfortunately, what she'd discovered was a lot more than stained wallpaper.

The old house had dry rot, a cracked foundation, a roof that crumbled under the inspector's feet and warped floors. The electrical system needed an overhaul and the furnace was on its last legs.

She'd taken the contractor's bid to the bank and had spoken to her grandmother's "man of affairs," as Pearl called him. It was then Maggie had learned the sad truth about the Jefferson family fortune—or lack of it. And there had been no question of a loan, being as how none of the Jefferson women were gainfully employed.

Maybe Kyle could fix that with his business-etiquette seminars—assuming that he was still interested. She could develop her own curriculum and test it on his people. Then, using Stuart Computers as a reference, she could get other jobs.

It wasn't much, but right now it was all she had. Or it would be when she met him in a little while. She ought to make some notes.

Maggie sat at the white French Provincial desk of her youth, as she had countless evenings before, and got out yellowed three-hole-punched notebook paper. Eating her ham sandwich as she wrote—Pearl would be horrified—Maggie listed questions she had, specifically about the Japanese visitors. Kyle would probably need someone to help with that, and Maggie wanted that job, too.

At seven-thirty, she put her papers into her briefcase and opened the bedroom door. She'd reached the bottom of the stairs and had taken two steps into the foyer when her grandmother's voice stopped her.

"And just what are you doing out of your room, young lady?"

She'd forgotten that she'd been banished. Just in time, Maggie dropped her purse and briefcase, and shoved behind her. "I—I wanted a glass of water."

"Ruby, get the child her water. Your mother will bring it to you, Magnolia." Pearl frowned at the jeans Maggie wore, but refrained from commenting.

Maggie returned to her room and shoved the briefcase under her bed. How was she supposed to get out of the house? The last thing she wanted was a huge fuss, especially before she had a chance to talk with Kyle again.

As it was, she'd have to be careful that no one saw the two of them together, or her grandmother would find out something was afoot before Maggie was ready to tell her.

Boy, she wasn't looking forward to that.

There was a tap on her door. "Here's your water, Maggie."

"Sorry to disturb you, Mama."

Ruby handed her the glass. "This is plain silly, sending a grown woman to her room. I'm going to talk to your grandmother."

"No!"

Ruby turned, her eyebrows arched in surprise.

"I mean, let's not upset Grandmother. I'll catch up on my reading and turn in early."

"You're being very understanding."

Feeling guilty, Maggie nodded. "It's okay. Good night."

After listening to her mother's departing steps, Maggie crossed the room and unlocked her window. Before she could get the window open, she had to break the paint seal with the engraved letter opener she'd won in the fourth-grade spelling bee.

Poking her head outside, Maggie looked out onto the side yard and the huge old oak tree whose branches rubbed against the gutters.

The tree had grown since Maggie had first occupied her bedroom. She'd always thought that she could sneak out by climbing down the sturdy branches, but she wasn't much of a tree climber. She'd practiced once, making it to the fork at the trunk, but not jumping. The ground was a long way down and since she was only practicing, Maggie hadn't seen the point in risking a sprained ankle.

Unfortunately, she'd never had anything or anyone to sneak out for. No, she'd been a model Jefferson daughter, with only occasional episodes of backtalking, which her mother got blamed for as much as Maggie.

Maggie eyed her escape route. "I am too old to be climbing down trees." Never mind climbing back up. She'd worry about that later.

She tossed her purse and briefcase to the ground, then eyed the nearest branch. Unfortunately, the nearest branch wasn't all that thick or that near. Maybe it was because trees looked thinner with only the small leafy spring growth.

Maggie hiked herself onto the window ledge, resolutely looking at her target and not at the ground. Had her mother ever climbed down this tree? Probably. Maggie peered into the branches, searching for Ruby's initials.

"Coward," she admonished herself. "Think of the money." She poked her foot at some leaves, trying to remember how she'd climbed out nearly twenty years before.

At last, Maggie reached for one branch and eased out onto another, which creaked loud enough to be heard over Opal's TV, if anyone was listening. Maggie gingerly eased her way to the trunk and sat, feeling accomplished, until she remembered that this was as far as she'd ever gotten.

KYLE PARKED HIS CAR down the street from the Jefferson house, hoping no one would recognize him. He had to talk to Maggie again, but had no idea where the

Garthwhiddle place was. His plan was to catch her as she left—assuming she still planned to meet him.

So much depended on her cooperation. That grandmother of hers had gone off the deep end. Maggie would have to defy her to work with him, which meant that she was in a really excellent negotiating position and was enough of a businesswoman to know it. He wondered what she'd ask for. He'd heard the Jeffersons were loaded, so it wouldn't be money.

Probably another Jefferson monument. They'd pretty much used up things to name in the town.

Kyle reached the Indian hawthorn at the edge of the Jefferson property. There wasn't a car visible in the cracked driveway and he hoped Maggie hadn't already left. He was trying to decide what to do when he heard a nearby rustling.

A guard dog? That would be his luck.

About the time he figured out that the sound was coming from the big old oak tree next to the house, he caught sight of someone scooting along a branch.

When he realized it was Maggie, he grinned. She'd probably climbed out her bedroom a hundred times before. He waited, but when he didn't hear anything more, he walked around the edge of the bushes and across the lawn toward the tree.

No sign of Maggie, but he found her purse and a briefcase.

He stared up into the tree. "Maggie?" he whispered. "Are you up there?"

"Kyle? You're supposed to be at the Garthwhiddle place."

"I would be if I could find it. There aren't any Garth-whiddles in the phone book."

"Of course not. They're all dead. But everybody knows where Dogwood Hill is."

Everyone who'd grown up in Jeffersonville. "I don't."

"You could have asked someone."

"I did! But nobody *I* know knows any Garthwhid-dles."

"Figures."

He stared up at her. She was a long way up. "Well, come down and you can show me where the place is."

Silence. "Maggie?"

"I don't know how to get down."

"*Climb* down."

"On *what?* I don't see any branches from here to the ground."

"How do you usually get down?"

"I take the stairs and walk out the front door," she snapped.

He grinned. "What did you do when you were a kid?"

"Took the stairs and walked out the front door."

Kyle laughed and Maggie shushed him.

"Have you got a ladder somewhere around here?" he asked.

"Who knows?" She sounded disgusted.

"I'll go look in the garage." Kyle was already headed in that direction when Maggie's hushed warning floated down to him.

"Watch out for the—"

Kyle's toe bumped up against something. As he lost his balance, he grabbed for the downspout at the side of the house. Screeching, it gave way and he fell across a container that sounded as if it was filled with glass, some of which was now broken.

"—jelly jars."

Kyle heard footsteps and froze, then scrambled into the shadows as the screen door opened.

"Reeow!"

The sound came from high up in the tree, about where he judged Maggie to be sitting.

"Reoooow!"

"It's the van Hornes' cat again," he heard Pearl Jefferson say. "Opal, I'm telling you, they don't keep their cat inside any better than they do those boys of theirs."

The door closed again, but Maggie's grandmother continued her harangue against the van Horne boys. "I don't know why she won't take my advice about sending them to military school. That'll take the vinegar out of them."

Kyle limped toward the tree. "Here, kitty, kitty."

"Very funny. Are you okay?"

"Banged up my shin and scraped my hand." In the waning light, he checked his palm. "Yeah, I'm spilling Yankee blood on your lawn."

"Grandmother will be so pleased."

He laughed up at her, definitely hoping he'd get a chance to know her better. "Hey, we need to get you down."

Hugging the tree, Maggie peered around her, then shook her head. "This was a bad idea. How about we try again tomorrow evening? I'll leave by the front door."

No. Kyle didn't want her thinking too much about meeting him. Too much thinking led to second thoughts. "Just ease yourself off the branch and let go. I'll break your fall."

"That's not all you'll break."

"And think how happy *that* will make your grandmother."

She stared down at him. "You must really want that computer chip."

"Yes, ma'am."

"Okay." And just like that, she jumped.

Kyle barely had time to brace himself before the impact, which carried them both to the ground.

They lay there, chest to chest, panting in the purpling twilight.

It was a position Kyle normally liked to be in with a woman. "You could have warned me!"

"I was afraid I'd lose my nerve," Maggie confessed with appealing honesty. "Are...are you hurt?"

Probably. "I'm still numb. I'll let you know."

"I'm sorry."

As feeling gradually returned to his extremities, Kyle became aware of the silky curtain of brown hair on either side of his head and the sweet smell that now enveloped him. He inhaled, which involved additional wonderful sensations as the soft weight of Maggie's body settled onto his.

He'd broken their fall with one arm—his wrist was

already beginning to throb—but the other was draped across Maggie's lower back.

Skin. He felt skin. Maggie's skin.

Her sweater had ridden up her rib cage and his hand was just below the edge.

Smooth, velvety skin.

She propped herself off his chest, at the same time pressing her lower body into his.

He gasped. Nothing was numb anymore and in two seconds she'd know it.

Just in time, she rocked back on her knees and tugged her sweater down. "I'm fine, in case you wondered."

He rolled to his side. "You felt fine." His voice sounded funny in a frustrated, teenagerish way.

She poked him with her toe. "Are you sure you're okay?"

Kyle moaned, just for the sympathy factor. Any compassion he could garner would help the cause.

"Where's your car?" an obviously unsympathetic Maggie asked. "I can't take my grandmother's. They'll hear it now, for sure."

He got to his feet. "My car's down the block."

"This block?" Her breath hissed between her teeth. "Well, let's go then."

FEELING SHAKY, Maggie gathered her purse and briefcase. She wanted like anything to blame her jitteriness on jumping out of the tree, but was afraid the blame lay squarely with the man who was now brushing at the grass stains on his pants.

She could still feel the imprint of his body beneath hers and it was causing an actual ache deep within her. She wanted to forget her grandmother and his socially inept employees and go someplace where she could press her body against his for as long as she wanted.

It didn't help that the old Garthwhiddle property was now the premier make-out spot in Jeffersonville.

Maggie, you've been deprived of male company for entirely too long. That was it. That was all it could be.

She and Kyle hurried down the block to his bright red car. Maggie only hoped no one on the street had seen it, but that was extremely unlikely. What had he been thinking?

There was no sense worrying about it now. Still, she tucked her hair into the neckline of her sweater and ducked her head. Maybe her jeans would fool people, since everyone knew the Jefferson women always wore skirts.

"Where to?" Kyle asked after he'd pulled away from the curb as quietly as a sports car could.

At least he hadn't peeled rubber as he had the day before.

Maggie directed him to the outskirts of Jeffersonville. As they drove through town, she kept her hand over her face and avoided eye contact with the statue of LaRue Jefferson in the center of Jefferson Square.

"Turn here. Another ten minutes or so and you'll see the gates to an old plantation-style house. That's the Garthwhiddle place. We don't need to go that far. I just had to think of someplace quick where we wouldn't be seen together." Babble, babble, babble. Why had she lost all her nerve around him?

Kyle pulled off the road. "At least I'll know where it is for future reference."

Maggie swallowed. "Exactly."

He glanced at her and turned off the engine. "I hope that means you're on my side."

Maggie didn't like the idea of taking sides. "It means that our conversation was interrupted and I'd like to finish it."

"Shall we get out of the car, or—"

"The mosquitoes would eat us alive."

"Right." He shifted in the leather seat so that he was facing her.

Maggie allowed herself a moment to rethink her decision to remain in such close proximity to Kyle Stuart. A two-seater sports car was vastly more intimate than a porch swing. And leather was so much more comfortable than wooden slats. And much more sensuous.

Drawing a deep breath to steady herself, Maggie caught the leather scent of the car, and the underlying masculine essence Kyle had brought to it.

It was so alien from the talcum-powder smell that permeated her grandmother's Cadillac. So male...so wonderfully male. Maggie's toes curled.

Kyle cleared his throat, drawing her attention to the open-neck denim shirt he wore and the fact that, in this light at least, the color exactly matched his eyes.

"You must have questions?" he asked.

You're sure you're not seeing anyone? "Yes." Maggie tucked her hair behind her ear. "You're saying—"

"Just a minute." Kyle's fingers fiddled with her hair. "Looks like a piece of bark." He pulled it out, rolled down his window a crack and flicked the bark outside.

Maggie's lungs felt tight and wouldn't expand enough for her to breathe. She stared at him, searching for anything on him that would let her touch him back. Her lips were dry and she licked them.

"Sorry, I didn't mean to interrupt." He smiled easily, but since Maggie was staring at his eyes, she knew it was only a surface smile.

Okay. She could do this. It was important to him. It was important to her. Maggie flipped open her briefcase and withdrew the girlish notebook paper. "As I understand the situation, you want to hire me to conduct business-etiquette seminars for your employees." She put a subtle emphasis on "hire" to let him know she expected to be compensated.

"Yes, and specifically prepare them for dealing with the Japanese."

That would take some research. She'd always been intrigued with the idea of international business relations. She'd look forward to that aspect of the job. "Tell me about the Japanese company."

Maggie listened as Kyle talked about that chip again and why the Japanese were so interested in the community.

"They seem awfully eager to fit in," she said.

"It makes sense, doesn't it? Their children will be going to our schools, they'll be living side by side with us. Why wouldn't they be concerned?" Kyle looked over at her. "So how about it? Will you help me convince your grandmother to agree to a truce?"

Maggie looked back at him, straight into his true-blue eyes. "I think we can do a lot better than a truce."

5

FOR A SECOND, KYLE LOST track of the conversation. The way Maggie was looking at him...southern women knew how to say a lot without words. But the words weren't bad, either. "Better than a truce? What do you mean?"

"I've spent the last several months job hunting and I know what it's like out there. It would be in Jeffersonville's best interests to keep Stuart Computers here. If we can convince my grandmother that we're collaborating for the sake of the town, then we might have a shot." She raised an eyebrow. "It's all in the approach."

Kyle closed his eyes and leaned against the headrest. "Does this mean you're going to help me?"

"Of course I'm going to help you. We are now negotiating the extent of that help."

Oh, the relief. He exhaled. "Maggie, thanks. Thank you, thank you, thank you."

"We've got some *major* obstacles ahead of us." She turned on the car's map light, closed her briefcase and used the top as a desk to write on. "First, we've got to persuade my family to see you. I'll have to convince them that they're making a personal sacrifice for the good of Jeffersonville. Grandmother loves personal sacrifices."

Maggie jotted down notes as she talked. Kyle liked watching her write. He pretty much liked everything about her. He would have still liked her even if she'd told him to take a hike.

"You've never formally been introduced to my grandmother, have you?"

"No."

"We'll have to fix that." She continued writing. "You mentioned something about a pavilion?"

"Yes. It rained on the Fourth of July last year, and I thought a covered area would make a great addition to the park. Maybe a place for an old-fashioned town picnic with bands and that sort of thing."

"I like that." She smiled and Kyle smiled, too.

"Okay," she continued, "that can be your reason for calling—you want to ask her opinion about the pavilion. She's president of the Jeffersonville Historical Society and you can ask her if Jeffersonville had a pavilion like that in the past."

Maggie was good. But Kyle was going to build the thing no matter what Pearl Jefferson thought. "Won't she wonder why I'm calling on her after all these years?"

He couldn't swear to it, but he thought Maggie was blushing.

"I'll...tell her something," she mumbled. "Now, about you. What's your background?" She gazed at him, pencil poised.

He told her a little about himself, which she used to

question him further. He felt as though he was interviewing for a job.

After several minutes, Maggie looked at her notes and sighed. "It's too bad that you don't have any relatives in the South."

"Well, pardon me for being from Pennsylvania."

"No, I meant that it would be easier to find some connection—someone my grandmother knows." She tapped her pen. "Why did you come to Jeffersonville, anyway?"

"It's near Atlanta and several communications companies had relocated there, for one thing. The first time I saw Georgia was when I went to Savannah for my cousin's wedding, and I—"

"You have cousins in Savannah?"

"No, my cousin married a woman from there. They still live there, come to think of it."

Maggie threw her hands up. "Haven't I just been asking you if you have relatives in the South?"

"He's not from the South."

"Who did he marry? What was her family name?"

"I don't know what her name was! We're not that close."

The concept of a family not being close apparently took Maggie a moment to absorb. "Can you find out her maiden name?"

"I guess." It must be important. "I'll ask my mother."

"Please do." Maggie continued writing. "It's odd, though, that your cousin stayed in Savannah with her people."

"Her family owns a big department store and my cousin went to work for them. I remember because we all got fitted for our tuxedos there," Kyle said.

"What was the name of the store?" Maggie asked, as he'd known she would.

"Maggie—it was back when I was in college!"

"Think!"

Kyle rubbed his forehead. "It was a white building downtown...and I got the impression that it was a big deal, you know, a real ritzy place." He remembered his grandmother using a pretty brass-and-glass outside elevator to get to the upper floors. He described it to Maggie and her eyes got big.

"That's Carlyle's! You're related to the department store Carlyles!"

"I'm not, my cousin—"

"Do they have children?"

"I *think* so."

She sat back, a satisfied look on her face. "Blood kin to the department store Carlyles. You're in." She beamed at him.

Kyle couldn't believe all this was so important, but if Maggie said it was, then it was.

She gathered her papers and put them back into her briefcase. "It might take me a few days to arrange a meeting. You should bone up on your family history."

Kyle laughed, though he knew she was serious. He also realized he wanted to know more about her. "Now tell me about your family history and the founding of Jeffersonville. Shouldn't I know about it before I meet your grandmother?"

MAGGIE'S FAMILY history was…interesting. She wasn't certain how much of it she wanted him to know.

"Sapphira, my great-great-grandmother, was a Yankee."

"So you're blood kin to Yankees. My, my."

Maggie laughed. "You might say Jeffersonville was founded because of the family silver, which comes from Sapphira's mama. They were in Philadelphia during the War of Northern Aggression."

The South's name for the Civil War brought a smile to Kyle's face. "A fellow Pennsylvanian."

"Good point." Maggie made a note.

"I'm surprised you've still got the silver. Wasn't she forced to sell it to support the family?"

Maggie felt a few twinges of guilt, since she'd thought of doing that very thing. "Who could afford to buy it after the war? Anyway, Sapphira had dutifully returned home to nurse her sick mother. Unfortunately, because she stayed on at home when LaRue Jefferson went off to fight in the war, it looked like she'd bolted for the North rather than supported the South."

"And people had a problem with that?" Kyle asked.

"Yes. It caused a lot of hard feelings from the citizens of Atlanta." Maggie shrugged. "LaRue survived and when Sapphira returned to Georgia, she brought back actual money—gold—inherited from her family. Atlanta society ostracized her. And LaRue refused to tolerate rudeness to his wife."

"And so they founded their own town," Kyle concluded.

"Right. Thus you have the story of Jeffersonville."

She lightly dismissed the rest of the family history that had been drummed into her since birth.

Sapphira had never recovered from her hurt and had instilled an unyielding sense of pride in her daughter, Beryl, a spinster, who had in turn instructed her nieces Opal and Pearl. The heavy ties of family honor and responsibility to the community the Jeffersons had founded had begun to unravel around Ruby, Maggie's mother, and Coral, Opal's daughter. Ruby abdicated her responsibility as the next female head of the Jefferson household in favor of Pearl, who hadn't wanted to relinquish her role as matriarch anyway. Coral was a matron at a home for unwed mothers, which Pearl and Opal referred to as "missionary work."

"Tell me why you don't you have a jewel name like the others?" Kyle asked suddenly.

Maggie fastened her briefcase and set it on the floor at her feet. "That was my mother's doing. You can probably tell that she has a rebellious streak in her."

"She didn't stray too far from home."

"Well, at one time she did. She went to college, she marched, she protested, she communed."

"Communed?"

"You know, vegetarian farms where everyone has names like Rainbow, Cloud and Freedom."

"And Magnolia?"

Maggie found it difficult to talk about her mother's wilder days since she didn't know much about them and didn't understand what she did know. "My father went off to Vietnam and never came back. That's all I know about him. I don't even know his name—his real name. Rather ironic, considering how you were grilled about your family."

"I didn't mind."

Of course not, he knew *all* the branches of his family tree. "Mother came back here, where I was born. She had a little rebellion left in her and named me Magnolia, intending to call me Maggie. According to her baby-name book, Maggie is a Greek name, meaning pearl."

A smile stole across Kyle's face as he slowly nodded. "Very clever." He shifted in the seat, bringing him several inches closer.

Maggie didn't know if it was on purpose or not. "I didn't used to think so. I hated my name. But I suppose Mother was trying to show me that I could be an individual, yet still have ties to family tradition."

"Magnolia. A flower of the South." He gazed at her, studying her face. "It suits you."

Maggie felt herself falling under the power of his intense blue gaze. She'd fought it subconsciously all evening. She must be tired. "Does it?"

"Uh-huh."

The atmosphere in the car changed. Maggie felt it, and knew she should suggest they leave, but the words remained unsaid, evaporated by the rising heat within her.

It was raw desire. Raw, because she didn't know this man well enough to be feeling this way about him.

It wasn't real. It wouldn't last. Strangely, she didn't care.

Her senses became heightened. She noticed his eyebrows, how one was slightly higher than the other, the texture of his skin, the crisp lines of his sideburns, the shape of his ears, the creases in his neck, the nicely shaped mouth and the little scar on his chin. She watched his pupils contract and his lips part.

"You shouldn't look at me like that," he whispered.

"Like what?" But she knew.

He moved closer. "As though..." She moved closer. "You want—"

The rest of the sentence was lost as he kissed her.

Maggie felt as though she'd never been kissed before. Something within her responded in a new way—as if a key had turned and unlocked her heart.

Her hands cradled the sides of Kyle's face, keeping him close as their mouths met and retreated before fusing together. She felt the heat within her spread outward and envelop them both.

Did he sense it? Did he feel anything the way she did? Could he tell that this was no simple kiss?

Potent feelings bombarded Maggie. She wanted to absorb his scent and taste, and wanted to imprint hers on him so that no other woman would ever truly be his. She wanted to claw and bite and brand.

The strength of these wild and primitive longings shocked her. She'd only met him, yet something inside her—something she had no idea existed—was responding to him.

Kyle pulled away, looking as dazed as she felt. "Maggie—"

She kissed him so he wouldn't talk, so she wouldn't

have to explain—and simply because she had to feel his mouth against hers once more.

The dim map light in the car grew brighter.

And brighter.

They stilled. Headlights. Headlights attached to a car that turned off the main highway and came straight toward them.

"Oh, no!" Maggie clutched at Kyle's arm. "We can't be seen together. It'll ruin everything."

"Keep your head down. I'll deal with them if they stop." He ran a hand through his hair and muttered, "I haven't been in *this* situation in a while."

"The map light! They can see us. Turn it off."

Kyle did, but Maggie knew it was probably too late. They'd already been seen for sure. Word would get back to her grandmother, who'd never agree to any collaboration.

The car slowed as it approached, and Maggie's heart pounded even harder than it had the previous few minutes.

But the car continued down the gravel road toward the Garthwhiddle place.

Maggie exhaled.

"The driver gave me a thumbs-up as he passed," Kyle said.

"Did you recognize him?"

"No, it was some kid. Probably, ah, looking for a little privacy."

"The Garthwhiddle place is popular for...privacy." She couldn't meet his eyes. What was she going to say to him?

"Maggie?" He slipped his arm around her shoulders, but she shrugged it off.

"Would you please take me home now?" she whispered, still not looking at him.

She could feel him studying her. "Okay," he said softly. He put on his seat belt and started the car.

Maggie was grateful that he hadn't said anything more. She clicked her seat belt into place and rested her face against the cool glass. They'd fogged up the windows and Kyle turned up the air conditioner. She couldn't imagine what he must be thinking of her. She didn't know what to think of herself.

MAGGIE PROBABLY THOUGHT he was an oversexed jerk.

What had he been *thinking*? Kyle berated himself. Well, he'd been thinking of her skin, and her eyes, and her hair, and her lips, and her scent and especially the take-me-now expression on her face—which he may have imagined.

Except...except there was the matter of her very enthusiastic response...

No, no exceptions. This was very, very bad and he'd have to think of a very, very good apology.

Did he have some latent self-destruct wish?

Without Maggie's help, he had no hope with the Japanese—yet had he been thinking of the Japanese when he was kissing her?

Kissing her... Even now his mouth remembered the feel of hers.

He could kiss her forever. Touch her forever. Make love to her forever...

HE PROBABLY NEVER WANTED to see her again, Maggie thought, sneaking a glance at the silent man who drove her home. He hadn't said a word. He was probably too disgusted.

And he wanted her to teach business etiquette! Maggie stifled a moan and winced. Lesson number one: keep business and pleasure separate.

What if...what if he no longer wanted to hire her? What had she been thinking? This was the first—and only—certain opportunity she'd had to make money in months. And the way she'd thrown herself at him, what choice did he have but to kiss her back or embarrass her?

The statue of LaRue Jefferson looked sternly down upon them as Kyle drove past.

Maggie's home was only a few minutes away. She desperately struggled for something to say, but Kyle beat her to it.

"Maggie, I've been trying to think of what to say to you. And the truth is, I don't know what to say."

He glanced at her at the same moment she darted a look at him. They both looked away immediately.

Kyle was going to fire her. They turned onto Jefferson Boulevard and Maggie waited for the ax to fall. "Better stop the car here," she said.

Kyle pulled over to the curb. "I hope I haven't jeopardized our working relationship," he said, "but I'm afraid I have. I can tell you're uncomfortable and I want to reassure you that you don't have to be. I don't make a habit of ravishing southern belles." He smiled weakly.

Maggie met his rueful gaze and realized that he wasn't going to fire her. In fact, he was taking full responsibility for their "encounter." It would be so easy to let him.

"Please don't apologize. I-I'm the one who suggested we meet at Jeffersonville's favorite make-out spot." *S-o-o-o professional, Maggie.* "I think under the circumstances, you showed remarkable restraint. Let's just call this a little momentary craziness and move on."

He looked as though he wanted to say more, but simply nodded.

"I'd better walk from here." She opened the car door.

"I'm coming with you."

Before Maggie could object, Kyle was at the passenger-side door, waiting while she gathered her things.

"How are you getting back into the house?" he asked.

"Front door. I'm hoping they're all in their rooms by now. Opal will have the television on full blast, so I should be able to slip in without anybody knowing."

They reached the edge of the Indian hawthorn. "Shall I call you?" Kyle asked.

"I'll call you. It'll be easier."

He stuck his hands in his back pockets. "Okay."

They nodded awkwardly at each other, and Maggie crept up the front walk. She climbed the wooden porch steps at the far left side so they wouldn't creak.

When she reached the front door, she eased open the screen. The spring hummed, but there weren't any squeaks. Through the lace curtains at the windows, Maggie saw a grayish glow. Opal's TV.

Easing her key into the lock, Maggie opened the front door enough to get her arm through and felt around for the chain. Why they used the chain, she didn't know, since it took only a moment to release. She remembered a time when they hadn't bothered to lock their doors.

That was before the Stuart Computer people moved to Jeffersonville and Pearl became convinced that the Jefferson family treasures were in jeopardy.

Maggie stepped inside and relocked the door.

The hall light came on. "And just where have you been?"

Maggie dropped her briefcase. Before her stood the three Jefferson Jewels.

Pearl, regal in a full-length purple velour robe, stood with her arms crossed and her face stern.

Ruby, holding a baseball bat, wore an oversize pink T-shirt from the "Walk for a Cure" breast cancer fund-raiser two years ago.

Opal wore a mauve silk peignoir edged in feathers from Victoria's Secret, a chin strap and an olive green mud pack designed to close her pores.

"I've been...out," Maggie said.

They stared at her, then at one another. "She's been out with Mr. Stuart," Pearl said.

How did they know? The car?

"Oh, Maggie, you're glowing." Opal clasped her hands together.

"What do you mean, glowing?"

"I told you to be careful, Maggie," her mother said. "You were careful, weren't you?"

They all stared at her again.

Maggie felt her face heat. She didn't need to check in the hall mirror to know that if she hadn't been glowing before, she was now. "We were *talking*."

It was obvious that she was fooling no one.

"Maggie, no good can come of illicit love," Opal said sorrowfully.

"Or even licit love," Ruby grumbled.

"As if you'd know, Ruby," her mother said pointedly.

Ruby glared at her mother. "He was an *ordained* minister in the Church of Celestial Light."

"So where's the license?"

"Licenses are earthly proofs required by man, not by God."

"I think we're all getting *way* ahead of ourselves," Maggie interrupted the ancient argument.

"Maggie, don't ruin your future." Her mother set the bat against the wall. "You don't need a man."

"Well, *needing* a man and *wanting* a man—"

"Opal!" both Ruby and Pearl snapped.

Opal threw back her shoulders. "I shall retire to get my beauty sleep. Sloane and Summer are getting married tomorrow on 'Garner's Bay,' and I want to look my best." She flounced off to her room.

"That vile Yankee!" Pearl drew a breath. "He tried to seduce you, didn't he? Don't deny it."

"I do deny it!"

"Maggie, you've got a good education," her mother said. "Don't waste it."

"Mama, Grandmother." Maggie held first her mother's hand, then her grandmother's, and squeezed. "I know I've got an education and I'm trying to use it. Kyle wants me to conduct business-etiquette seminars for his employees, but you're being so stubborn and ungracious that I can't discuss it here." She decided not to mention the Japanese at this point.

"I forbid you to step foot in that building and tutor his ill-bred employees," Pearl pronounced.

"Why?"

"Because Mr. Stuart is not someone with whom you should associate."

"Why?" Maggie asked again.

Pearl's mouth opened and closed and she turned to Ruby. "You see the influence you've had on your daughter?"

"Well, I hope so," Ruby said.

Pearl's nostrils flared. "Magnolia, how can you bear to have anything to do with that man after the slights to which he's subjected us?"

"Grandmother, did you ever ask him to call?"

"Everyone knows we're at home each day during tea."

"Maybe he didn't think he'd be welcome. Maybe he thought he'd be run off the porch with a broom!"

Pearl's cheeks pinkened.

Ruby cackled. "She's got you there."

Maggie pressed her advantage. "And now, when he needs someone to instruct his people in the ways of polite social and business interaction, did he go to Atlanta? Did he go to New York? Did he go someplace else where they have companies that do that sort of thing? No. He came to *us*." She paused, then delivered the zinger. "He came to us because he thought we were the most qualified—and you ran him off the porch with a broom."

Pearl wilted before her eyes. She grabbed Ruby's arm for support. "Oh, dear. We must...we must make amends."

Ruby nodded, watching Maggie carefully.

"Magnolia, do you think Mr. Stuart would accept an invitation to tea?"

Maggie tried to hide her satisfaction. "All I can do is ask."

6

HE'D BEEN FORMALLY invited to tea. Kyle reknotted his tie, then ripped it off and grabbed another.

He hadn't been this nervous since...he couldn't remember when he'd ever been this nervous.

How Maggie had wangled the tea invitation, Kyle didn't know, but his respect for her diplomatic abilities ratcheted up another notch.

It was Sunday afternoon, and Kyle would normally be outside playing softball on a day as balmy as this one.

He lived in the penthouse he'd had built on the top floor of the Stuart building. From the window, he could see into the park where Mitch and the others were playing ball.

Kyle had made participating on the company team a requirement because they were spending too much time inside.

Nobody complained anymore.

Turning away from the window, he looked over the notes his mother had given him on his family one more time and prepared for the final exam.

AT PRECISELY FOUR O'CLOCK, a rap sounded on the front door.

"That will be Mr. Stuart. He's prompt, I'll give him that. You may proceed to the door, Magnolia."

Conscious that Ruby and Pearl were watching, Maggie walked sedately toward the front door, though her heart pounded as if she'd just run a marathon.

This would be the first time she'd been face-to-face with Kyle since the night she'd climbed out the window.

She still couldn't believe the feelings that had been unleashed that night. Maggie was well aware of her family's fertility curse and had no intention of becoming an unwed mother. In fact, it was her secret fear that she would end up back here in the old house, pregnant and abandoned by the man in her life just the way they'd all been. And look at her—she was already back living at home.

Shuddering, she pasted on a smile, stopped to check it in the mirror over the credenza, inhaled and opened the door.

She did not exhale.

Kyle stood there and she was struck dumb. Every fiber of her being screamed that this was the man who should perpetuate the Jefferson line.

"Wow." She sighed, finally remembering to breathe again.

"So I pass inspection?" He held his arms out and turned around, the very picture of success.

"Oh, yes." She leaned on the door, giving her suddenly weak knees some much needed support.

"Maggie?"

"Yes?" she breathed, conscious of sounding faintly like Opal.

"Should I come in now? Are they ready for me?"

I'm ready for you, too. She stood to one side, stunned by her forceful and apparently uncontrollable reaction to him. For the first time, Maggie understood how someone could love foolishly, extravagantly and unwisely.

Kyle followed Maggie into the drawing room, where she noticed that Opal had joined the tableau. The Jefferson Jewels were in their proper setting.

Maggie watched their faces as they caught sight of him. Though her grandmother had already seen him, her eyes widened and she returned her cup to its saucer. Her mother stopped quilting.

Opal held her head at the angle she said showed her profile to its best advantage. This meant that unless she was seated on the right—and she never was—she appeared to face away from visitors.

Maggie introduced him, remembering doing so when he was pretending to be Mitchell McCormick. No one mentioned that and Maggie wasn't about to.

"Come sit beside me, Mr. Stuart." Opal patted the sofa.

Kyle sat next to her and Opal preened.

Maggie suddenly didn't like the idea of sharing Kyle.

"Magnolia tells us you're kin to the department store Carlyles," Pearl began.

"My cousin's wife's family," Kyle confirmed. "Robert is the store's vice president now."

"How very nice for him."

"Carlyle's is a lovely store," Opal added. "We receive their Christmas catalog."

"And how about your people?" Pearl asked.

With an amused look at an uneasy Maggie, Kyle traced his lineage for her grandmother and great-aunt. Even her mother, for all her scoffing of tradition, listened closely.

He'd obviously done his homework.

Bloodlines were discussed as though they were horse trading, Maggie thought, becoming impatient. Why was where a person came from so much more important than who that person was? Were they all shallow deep down inside? she asked herself, ignoring the way that sounded.

Kyle was holding his own. He flirted with Opal, deferred to Pearl and exchanged political salvos with Ruby. He was quite at ease with all the social graces.

And probably the fates and muses, as well.

Maggie was half listening as she waited for an opportunity to introduce the pavilion and the etiquette seminars and missed the turn the questions took. By the time she returned her full attention to the conversation again, she was horrified to realize that Kyle was being expertly grilled on his aspirations and the financial well-being of his family—as if he was a potential suitor.

She intercepted a satisfied look between Pearl and Opal.

A potential suitor. That was exactly the way they were

thinking of him. Maggie felt as though she'd been doused with a pitcher of iced tea. This was humiliating.

"Kyle, tell them about your plans for the pavilion."

Four pairs of eyes—three brown, one blue—stared at her.

Pearl set her teacup in her saucer. "Maggie seems quite excited about your pavilion, Mr. Stuart."

A subtle rebuke for breaking into the conversation. Maggie stuffed a lemon cookie in her mouth.

She ate another lemon cookie as Kyle explained the plans, then concluded with, "I know you're the president of the Jeffersonville Historical Society, Mrs. Jefferson, so I thought you could tell me if Jeffersonville ever had a bandstand or outdoor pavilion before. If so, we could re-create it or model the new one after it."

"I think that's a perfectly lovely idea, Mr. Stuart." Pearl bestowed a smile on him.

Kyle set down his glass of tea and leaned forward. Even though she knew what was coming, Maggie had to admire the way he delivered the line.

"And I thought we'd call it Jefferson Pavilion—if that's all right with you."

"Oh, Mr. Stuart, isn't that just *precious* of you? Isn't that precious of him, Pearl?" Opal tittered.

"That's a very gracious gesture, Mr. Stuart," Pearl allowed as her lips tilted upward in satisfaction. She would look upon this as a victory.

Ruby stabbed her quilt. "Seems to me the money could be better used by the Atlanta Women's Shelter."

Kyle looked momentarily nonplussed, so Maggie stepped in. "Mama, families will use the pavilion, so it is a benefit to the community." Maggie glanced at Kyle. "I can even see it used as a forum for public speaking, or a gathering spot at the end of our parades and rallies." *Or demonstration marches.*

Ruby stopped quilting and Maggie knew she was visualizing Kyle's unbuilt pavilion as a convenient platform for her causes. "Sounds good. Go for it."

Pearl cleared her throat. "I'll study my records and see what I can find, Mr. Stuart."

"Then it's settled. And you'll attend the dedication ceremony, of course?"

"Why, naturally."

"Great." Kyle sent one of his guaranteed-to-charm smiles around the room. "Since I hope we'll be working together, Maggie can keep you informed of the progress."

Maggie winced. This wasn't the time to bring up the seminars.

"I'm not altogether certain I know to what you are referring, Mr. Stuart."

"Now, Grandmother, I told you about the seminars, remember?"

"That's not at all settled." Pearl sipped her tea. "I'm not sure it's quite the thing for you to do."

Thing, schming. They needed the money.

"I agree," Kyle said to Maggie's surprise. "There is still some question over whether Maggie would be...welcome."

"Maggie not welcome?" Opal asked. "Why ever not?"

"The past relationship between your family and Stuart Computers has resulted in some hard feelings. And too, Maggie has no experience in this field. Without credentials—"

"Now, wait—"

Pearl held up her hand. "Magnolia is a Jefferson. That's the only credential she needs."

MAGGIE WALKED ACROSS the lobby of the Stuart Computers building toward the bank of elevators. It felt great to be back in the corporate world.

The building seemed so much bigger inside than it did from the outside. Metal, smoked glass and gray. All the Jeffersonville natives disparaged its modern look. Blinking lights, sleek surfaces and molded shapes. The lobby looked like the set of a science-fiction movie.

Maggie noted the chicly dressed businesswomen who strode purposefully in and out the revolving door which had just tried to eat her floral-print skirt. She planned to ditch the full skirts as soon as her grandmother got used to Maggie working at Stuart Computers.

She also noted that she recognized none of those chicly dressed businesswomen, and as far as she could tell, none of them recognized her.

The population of Jeffersonville had changed more than she'd realized—probably more than her grandmother had realized.

When Maggie got off the elevator, a blond receptionist directed her to an office near the end of the hall.

"You must be Maggie," a smiling, comfortably

dressed woman greeted her with breezy informality. "I'm Janet, Kyle's secretary." She gestured Maggie inside the room.

It was a large, but rather modest space. "Is this Kyle's office?" Maggie asked, looking around. "Where is he?"

"Oh, no!" Janet laughed. "This is *my* office. Kyle's is next door." She pointed toward a paneled wall with a connecting door. Maggie could hear voices. "He's just breaking the news about you to Mitch and the others."

The voices became louder, with one shouting above the rest, "That's the stupidest idea I've ever heard!"

Maggie stared at Janet, who suddenly discovered some papers on her desk requiring her immediate attention.

"I don't want to listen to some old biddy telling me how to drink tea!"

Masculine murmurs rumbled through the connecting door.

"I don't care what the Japanese do—that's not my job!"

Muffled footsteps crossed the room.

"Mitch!" Maggie recognized Kyle's voice before the door at the end of the hallway banged open.

Curious to see what the infamous Mitch looked like, Maggie stepped out of Janet's office.

"I've got work to do," declared a dark-haired man. Head lowered, he stalked down the hall, followed by several other men.

Maggie attempted to step back, but Janet was right behind her.

"Look out, Mitch!" Maggie heard before the man plowed into her, tramping on her foot and dislodging her navy pump.

He grunted an ungracious apology and walked on.

"Maggie, are you okay?" Janet exclaimed.

"More or less." Maggie rubbed her ankle as a white run snaked its way up her leg. Grabbing hold of the doorjamb, she repositioned her shoe.

"Watch it," one of the other men cautioned before brushing past.

Maggie stared at the backs of the retreating herd of men. They'd nearly run her over in their haste to escape.

"Hello, Maggie," said a familiar voice. Kyle gazed past her, unsmiling. "Welcome to Stuart Computers."

SHE SHOULD HAVE TRIPLED her fee, Maggie thought as Kyle introduced her to a roomful of sullen engineers.

After the episode outside his office that morning, Maggie supposed it was too much to expect wild enthusiasm, but she did expect politeness.

Everyone in the room obviously felt that what she had to say was a waste of time and they weren't afraid to show it.

The three women attending sat quietly and attentively, but Maggie suspected they agreed with their colleagues' assessment of her etiquette course and were being polite solely out of support for another woman.

At least they knew *how* to be polite. Maggie had her doubts about the others.

And by the end of the day, she had doubts about herself. At Kyle's suggestion, she emphasized the coming visit by the Japanese engineering firm and how she would point out the cultural differences in behavior. That way, she could introduce some basic etiquette principles without insulting the engineers.

Mitch challenged her as soon as Kyle left the room. "If somebody is offended by the way I hold my fork, then that's their problem and not mine." He sprawled in a conference-room chair and deliberately opened an electronics magazine.

Magnolia, direct descendant of LaRue Jefferson, was appalled by his behavior. However, Maggie, corporate trainer, wasn't fazed by his astonishing rudeness. Smiling, she walked around the large round conference table until she reached Mitch, then deftly confiscated his magazine and returned to her place. "You may have this back after class," she said, then immediately launched into her opening remarks.

"Hey! Gimme that back!" Mitch appeared dumbfounded.

"*After* class." Maggie stood her ground, knowing that if she gave in now, she'd never have their attention.

Mitch shoved his chair back. The legs caught on the carpet and the chair fell over. "This whole etiquette thing is stupid and I'm not wasting any more of my time." He glanced around, ready to lead a mutiny. "We'd be better off learning to speak their lingo!"

"Mr. Stuart felt strongly enough about the Matsuzaka visit to hire me," she said. "If you disagree with that decision, then you should take it up with him."

"That's *exactly* what I'm going to do!" Mitch shouted on his way out of the room.

Though she tried to ignore it, an uncomfortable tension remained for quite a while after Mitch's departure.

By the time she dismissed the class, Maggie was exhausted and frustrated.

The only thing that kept her from marching into Kyle's office and quitting was the sizable check he'd given her to cover a partial payment of her fee.

Well, not the only thing. If she quit, she'd never see him again. That might not be a bad thing, since seeing him was as disturbing as not seeing him. Not seeing him...ever again. No, that would be worse.

She'd better go to the bank and open a corporate account for Jefferson Protocol Consultants, as she was styling herself, before she could change her mind.

"I AM AWARE THAT I'm not a member of the Jeffersonville Country Club, Mr. Jamison. I have a copy of your letter declining my application in my files. However, I need to use the ballroom. Couldn't you make an exception in this instance?"

His irritation growing, Kyle listened to the man at the other end of the telephone connection blather on about rules and standards.

Bottom line: the old guard still wanted nothing to do with Stuart Computers.

Kyle disconnected the call before he said something

he'd regret. He'd run into dead ends all week. News of his détente with the Jeffersons apparently hadn't made any impact at all.

Obviously, Pearl's influence had been greatly exaggerated. The Jefferson Jewels were fake.

He hoped Maggie wasn't a fake, as well.

He'd tried sitting in on one of her sessions, but couldn't concentrate on what she was saying. From the way her eyes kept returning to his, he knew he made her uneasy.

Was it in the same way *she* made *him* uneasy? Kyle couldn't remember the last time a woman had gotten under his skin the way Maggie Jefferson had. And he couldn't figure out how. There was just *something* about her that attracted him. Something he found difficult to ignore. Something he didn't *want* to ignore.

Raised voices sounded in the outside hallway.

Now what?

"Kyle?" Maggie, a flustered Janet trying to restrain her, burst into his office. "I have *had* it with Mitchell McCormick!"

"It's okay, Janet."

Rolling her eyes, Janet shut the door.

"He's impossible!" Maggie shouted, looking flushed and sparkly eyed. "They're all impossible! I can't believe they'd act this way if they truly knew how important this visit is! Haven't you told them?"

The injustice of her accusation, coming right after his chat with Jamison, made him lose his temper. "*Yes*, I've told them!" Kyle stood and slammed the phone book on his desk. "And what is with this hick town of yours?

No one will cooperate with me. If your grandmother is such a big deal, then why hasn't she spread the word that I'm not Yankee scum anymore?''

Maggie marched over to the desk. ''I am certain that any difficulties you're having with Jeffersonville are entirely of your own making!''

Kyle leaned forward, planting his fists on his desk. ''If you were the hotshot corporate trainer you claim to be, you'd know how to handle somebody like Mitch.''

She dropped her fists on his desk, too. ''*Some*body like Mitch would have been fired long ago.''

''Like you were?''

He shouldn't have said that, he realized even as the words left his mouth.

Maggie, eyes wide, whirled and headed for the door.

''Maggie, I'm sorry.'' Kyle ran after her, but she didn't slow down.

''Maggie.'' He grabbed her elbow.

''Let go of me.'' She jerked her arm.

''No.'' He jerked back and she stumbled against him, soft and warm.

He heard her gasp, but all he saw were her parted lips before he covered them with his own.

His body reacted instantly, reminding him of the stolen moments in his car—images he'd been suppressing for over a week. A long week. A week in which he'd been tantalized with glimpses of her as she'd moved about the building.

A week when every time they made eye contact, they each looked quickly away. And he knew she was thinking about the kiss and he was thinking about the kiss and knowing he shouldn't be thinking about it. But he couldn't stop.

And now he was kissing her and it was even better than before.

"Maggie," he groaned against her mouth, when he meant to say, *I was going out of my mind and hoped you wanted to kiss me as much as I wanted to kiss you.*

"Oh, Kyle," she groaned back, but what she probably meant was *ditto.*

He wrapped his arms around her waist and lifted her off the ground in an effort to get as close as humanly possible to her.

But there was another way, a much better way—a way he wanted to try soon. Maybe now.

"Let—me lock the—door," he managed to whisper between kisses.

He set her down, dragged in much-needed oxygen and reached for the doorknob.

It jammed him in the hand as the door was opened from the other side.

"Hey, sorry about that." Mitch walked into the office. "Janet said I should come talk to you, so here I am."

"Yes, here you are." Kyle shook his hand, the pain proving to be an effective libido killer.

"So what's up?" Mitch asked.

"Nothing anymore," Kyle muttered under his breath.

Maggie looked flushed and wild-eyed—about the same as she'd looked when she was hopping mad.

Kyle swallowed. Maybe she was still hopping mad, but mad or not, he had to talk with her.

There was definitely chemistry between them, even though they'd both been careful not to be alone together. Now Kyle was ready to try the opposite tactic—spend a few days and nights together and either build on the chemistry or let it fizzle. As soon as he could get rid of Mitch, he planned to discuss his idea with Maggie—in the penthouse.

"You've been giving Maggie trouble," Kyle said.

Mitch scowled. "She's wasting my time and everybody else's. Man, I could be working on a multimedia accelerator that will make everybody forget all about memory."

"We don't have time to wait for you to develop anything."

Mitch shot Maggie a triumphant look. "That's what I've been telling you—"

"*Mitch, shut up and listen.*"

Identical startled looks crossed the faces of both Maggie and Mitch.

"If we don't get that Japanese chip, we'll lose staff—we might even lose this building. That means you'll no longer have your lab and all your expensive toys."

Mitch stared at him and Kyle thought he might finally have gotten through to him.

"I think it's time for me to leave," Maggie said.

"Maggie—wait."

But she shook her head. "We'll talk later."

THE DAY HADN'T BEEN boring, she'd give it that.

Maggie was shaky from her confrontation with Kyle.

After spending an entire week telling herself she'd simply responded normally, if somewhat enthusiastically, to an attractive man—and now that she knew what to expect, she could control future responses to that same attractive man—Maggie was right back where she'd been last Friday night: frustrated.

At least she had a fairly good idea she wasn't alone. No, it wasn't a one-sided infatuation. So what did she intend to do about it?

As she wrestled the Cadillac out of the Stuart parking lot, Maggie asked herself why they shouldn't see each other socially. Date, in other words. True, they were working together, but that was just temporary. Their attraction might be just as temporary.

It wasn't as though Kyle was going to leave or anything. Where would he go? His business was in Jeffersonville. Yes, he might lose the building if he didn't get the chip, but it wasn't as if he was a soldier going off to war or a traveling salesman. He wouldn't leave her.

Maggie felt so relaxed when she decided to stop fighting her intense attraction toward Kyle that she turned the old Cadillac in the direction of the bank. Now that she had a corporate account, she was going to see about a loan. While she'd been stuck in the tree the other night, she'd gotten a good look at the section of roof over the second-best bedroom. It wouldn't last much longer.

"WHAT DO YOU MEAN, there isn't any money in the Jefferson Protocol Consultants account?" Maggie asked a balding Mr. Winthrop fifteen minutes later. "I deposited money just last week."

"And your mother withdrew it yesterday. We issued a cashier's check."

"You can't do that," Maggie said, dumbfounded.

Mr. Winthrop smiled patronizingly and laced his fingers together. "Oh, the bank can do many things, Miss Maggie. A cashier's check is simply—"

Miss Maggie interrupted him. "I *know* what a cashier's check is!"

She spun around and ran for the Cadillac. One thing about the full skirts, they allowed for running. Unfortunately, Maggie was back to wearing her short skirts, which meant raising both her skirt and several pairs of eyebrows of the Jeffersonville citizenry.

A short while later, she peeled into the driveway, leaving the car door open as she ran up the front steps and burst in upon the afternoon-tea tableau.

"Magnolia, a lady never—"

"Mama? What did you do with the cashier's check you got at the bank?"

"It's none of your concern, Maggie."

Maggie stood directly in front of her. "It is very much my concern. And I think you know that."

"Magnolia, do not use that tone of voice with your mother."

Maggie was too angry to conform to her grandmother's standards of behavior today. "What did you do with the cashier's check?"

Ruby serenely continued her quilting. "I sent it to the

Atlanta Women's Shelter, since Jeffersonville doesn't have one of its own."

"When?"

"Maggie, dear, you mustn't frown so, you'll get wrinkles," Opal said.

"Mama?"

"The letter went out in today's mail."

Ignoring the protests from Opal and Pearl, Maggie ran back to the car and drove to the post office.

They refused to relinquish the letter, so she had to go back to the bank to stop payment on the check.

"Oh, don't worry," Mr. Winthrop assured her. "I wouldn't have returned the check. There was enough money in your account to cover it."

Right then and there, Maggie dropped all pretense of Jefferson sweetness until Mr. Winthrop understood that Jefferson Protocol Consultants was a business account on which only Magnolia B. Jefferson had check-writing privileges.

It had taken quite a while before she could convince Mr. Winthrop that she intended to "bother her pretty little head" about this on a regular basis.

And then she had to go and tell her mother to call the Atlanta Women's Shelter and inform them that payment had been stopped on the check they'd soon receive.

Her mother didn't take the news well, but Maggie hadn't expected her to.

Ruby, Opal and Pearl were still gathered for afternoon tea, no doubt discussing Maggie's deplorable behavior.

"I will *not* call them," Ruby declared.

"Fine." Maggie wearily accepted a glass of iced tea from her grandmother. "I'll call them."

"How dare you!" Ruby had risen and glared at her daughter with the light of battle in her eyes.

"Mama, we can't afford any more of your generous contributions." Maggie knew that her mother routinely supported many women's causes. All her quilts were donated or sold and the proceeds given away.

"I happen to know that Kyle Stuart is paying you in hopes that the Jefferson aura will make him socially acceptable," Ruby said.

"Money?" Opal opened her eyes so wide her eyelashes nearly touched her painted eyebrows. "That man is giving our dear Maggie money?"

"Don't be vulgar," Pearl instructed, no doubt preparing for a lecture on mentioning filthy lucre at tea.

"Yes, money." Ruby leveled a let's-drop-the-pretense look at Maggie. "Which she tried to hide from us."

A knot formed in Maggie's stomach. She hated these confrontations. Pearl and Opal had put their heads together, no doubt plotting ways to launder the stain on the Jefferson reputation.

"That was my business account."

"Mr. Winthrop at the bank said it was all right."

"Mr. Winthrop was mistaken." Maggie was still furious with the bank manager. "There wasn't enough money in the household account to cover your check."

Ruby rolled her eyes and returned to her quilting.

"He'll just have to transfer money from the fund, since you're being so stingy and mean-spirited."

"There is no more trust fund, Mama."

"Of course there is," Ruby insisted in a louder voice. "Your great-grandparents set one up."

Pearl and Opal stopped talking to listen.

"It's empty," Maggie said, not knowing how her relatives would take the news.

"Nonsense, Magnolia. There's always been money." Pearl sounded as though she could barely bring herself to mention the word.

Maggie took a deep, fortifying breath. "You withdrew most of it to pay for my college expenses, remember?"

"But more always came in."

That was true, but Maggie wasn't up to explaining the concept of principle and interest income and what happened to income when there wasn't any more principle. "Yes, but not enough to make up what was spent."

"Mr. Winthrop has always given me money when I've asked him," Pearl said. "Are you telling me he gave me money that wasn't ours?"

Maggie stared into her grandmother's guileless brown eyes. "That was money I'd put in from my salary." Which was why she'd unexpectedly found herself without savings. "And I have no more salary."

A small furrow appeared between Pearl's eyebrows.

"Does this mean we should postpone the reception?" Opal asked.

Maggie trained her gaze on her grandmother and great-aunt. "What reception?"

Furrow smoothed, Pearl sipped tea. "The reception after the Jefferson Pavilion dedication." She replaced her cup in the saucer and daintily set it on the silver tray. "People will expect it. You should know that. Opal, call the club. We must reserve our date."

Maggie wanted to weep with frustration. "Grandmother, we don't have a club membership anymore."

"A Jefferson not a member of the Jeffersonville Country Club?"

"You quit."

"Oh, that." Pearl waved away Maggie's explanation. "I resign every time Jamison and I have a disagreement." He and her grandmother had disagreed often over who should and who should not be admitted to the Jeffersonville Country Club. "It keeps him in line. No one would want to belong if we weren't members."

"You haven't paid dues," Maggie reminded her. "So technically we *aren't* members."

"Oh." Her grandmother turned to Opal. "Make a note to reinstate our membership."

Maggie pressed fingers to her temple, trying to relieve the tightness of an incipient headache. "Perhaps now is not the time, Grandmother. We can't afford to sponsor the reception anyway."

"But we've planned the decorations!" Opal's lip trembled. "We were just discussing the menu."

"Perhaps we could plan a picnic in the park instead," Maggie said.

"I agree with Maggie." Unexpectedly, Ruby came to

her aid. "So it's decided. "We'll donate the money we would have spent on the reception to help Georgia's destitute women."

"We're destitute women!" Maggie raised her voice and that simply wasn't done in the Jefferson household.

Her head throbbed.

Three pairs of horrified eyes gazed in her direction.

"Magnolia! How dare you say such a thing!" Her grandmother spoke in a scandalized whisper.

"Because we—have—no—money." Maggie leaned forward and spoke as plainly as she could. "It's gone. All of it. And the house is falling apart and we can't afford to do a thing about it." She slumped.

"Sit up straight, Magnolia," her grandmother said automatically.

And just as automatically, Maggie straightened. "I never thought to question the family finances." And apparently, neither did Mr. Winthrop.

"But the reception...?" Opal's voice trailed off as Maggie shook her head.

"That's why I tried so hard to find another job, and why I sold my car and moved back here. It wasn't until I wanted to transfer money into the checking account that I learned the fund was so low. Even then, I assumed there must be another account somewhere." Maggie gestured, palms up. "Everything's gone."

"Everything?" Ruby smoothed the fabric of her quilt.

"Except what I've got in the account I just set up."

Ruby and Opal looked to Pearl for verification. Pearl stared off into the distance.

"So, yes, you'd better believe that I'm charging Kyle Stuart to conduct those seminars. I know you don't like it, but we need money to replace the entire roof," Maggie informed her grandmother, declining to catalog other necessary repairs.

"Why, I'm aware of the small leak upstairs, but surely that doesn't indicate an entire new—"

Rude or not, Maggie interrupted. "No more patching. It's time for a new roof. And you said yourself that we're living in a sacred trust. We have to take whatever steps necessary to preserve our heritage. Not only that, we can only use carpenters from the Heritage Society's approved list. They cost more."

She had her grandmother's complete attention. Anytime one dealt with the Heritage Society or ancestors or sacred trusts, they could count on Pearl's complete attention.

Maggie warmed to her theme. "Our ancestors struggled through wars and the Great Depression. Now we're fighting the ravages of time. I, for one, am ready to take on the challenge, just as you taught me, Grandmother."

She ought to be ashamed of herself, Maggie thought, noting the moisture forming in Pearl's eyes.

"Bless you, child," she said, touching a lace-edged hankie to the corner of one eye.

Ruby, dry-eyed, blinked once, then bent over her quilt.

"Grandmother, I know you've heard that Kyle Stuart is trying to organize some business entertainments. From what he told me today, I'd even go so far as to guess that you've been dropping a few hints around town to make it difficult for him. I thought we settled everything when he came to tea."

"Perhaps certain people in town are not as forgiving as we are," Pearl said, admitting nothing.

Opal glanced anxiously at her sister and crumbled the lemon cookie she'd been nibbling.

"Well, you'd better convince those certain people that they're going to have to let bygones be bygones." Maggie drew a deep breath. "Our future and the future of Jeffersonville is at stake." She explained about the Japanese visit. "Whether or not you like him, you have to admit that he provides most of the jobs in this town. Without Stuart Computers, people will leave Jeffersonville in droves."

Then she waited for her words to sink in. She honestly didn't know what to expect next. She should have broken the news to them more gently, but it was done now.

The clock chimed the quarter hour in the silence.

"A Jefferson has never backed down from a challenge." Pearl sniffed and tucked her handkerchief in her bodice. "You say Mr. Stuart is attempting to plan the entertainments by himself?"

Maggie nodded. "I'd hoped to convince him that he needs to hire a coordinator."

"You?" Ruby asked.

"That's right, Mama," Maggie replied evenly.

"And he'll pay you for that, too?"

"I certainly hope so. We need every penny we can get."

The Jewels looked at one another.

"Maggie shouldn't have to do everything by herself."

Pearl drew a deep breath. "That, Ruby, is precisely what I was thinking. After all, Jeffersonville's future is at stake." She brushed at Opal's lemon-cookie crumbs. "Magnolia, you may inform Mr. Stuart that we will oversee this visit."

7

MAGGIE KNOCKED ON Kyle's office door first thing the next morning. "I've got great news."

"So do I."

"You first." Grinning, she crossed the room, sat in the chair in front of his desk and crossed her legs.

Kyle stared at her legs. "We're going to celebrate."

"That's your good news?"

"Doesn't celebrating sound good to you? It sounds good to me."

She slipped the heel of her pump off and the shoe dangled from her toes. "So what are we celebrating?" Her foot flexed ever so slightly.

Kyle blinked at her foot. They had to have a reason? "Your good news."

She laughed, a throaty chuckle that vibrated up and down his spine. "You haven't heard my good news yet."

"Are you going to celebrate with me?"

"Sure."

"That sounds like good news to me." He stared at her, wishing she'd shut the door behind her. Wishing Janet would go for a cup of coffee or something.

"Grandmother has decided to help you with the Japanese. I don't think you'll have any more problems with the people of Jeffersonville." She looked pleased.

Japanese? Oh, yeah. Right. "That's nice."

"Kyle! Is that all you have to say?"

He closed his eyes, but he could still see her sitting in front of him. He could still see her skirt inching up her legs. "If I don't get you alone soon, I will drive my car across your lawn, park under that oak tree, stand on the hood, hoist myself onto the branch, climb over to your window, fling myself inside and have my way with you." He opened his eyes and gazed steadily into hers. "Do you understand?"

Her eyes had taken on a glazed look. Nodding, she stood and worked her heel back into her shoe.

"And?" Every nerve in his body waited for her answer.

"And when are we celebrating?"

He remembered to breathe. "Now?"

"I don't think so." But she didn't sound all that certain, he noted.

"Tonight? I'll cook." Was he crazy? He didn't cook.

"But...Grandmother wants you to come over tonight. To discuss...the, uh..." She trailed off because Kyle had rolled his chair from behind the desk, reached for her hand and was gently but insistently drawing her toward him. "I really think you should—"

"Then tomorrow night, or you'll have tire tracks on your lawn." He let her go, not because he wanted to, but because the door was open and Janet was at her desk and because people wandered in and out of his office at will.

"Okay." Maggie visibly wobbled as she headed toward the door.

"Oh, Maggie?"

She turned.

"Mitch understands now. You won't have any more trouble with him or the others."

MAGGIE REMAINED in a daze for the rest of the day. At tea, the Jewels were subdued, but had obviously spent a lot of time with their recipes and Opal's card file reviewing past entertaining triumphs.

Ruby's extensive experience of organizing marches and her work on political campaigns had been put to good use. A grand plan was in the making.

Maggie wasn't much help. She caught them giving her long looks, but she didn't care.

Kyle was coming over tonight, and tomorrow...they'd celebrate.

She knew what it meant and she welcomed it. She was a modern woman and she'd take modern precautions.

Unfortunately, she could protect everything but her heart, and she was afraid she'd already lost that to Kyle. Whenever she told herself that real and lasting love took time, her heart responded that it had taken all the time it needed.

Maggie was inclined to believe it.

When Kyle arrived to discuss the Japanese visit, Maggie paid no attention to what he said, but only the way he looked when he said it.

He even spoke to her once—she saw his mouth move. His mouth... She sighed.

Her mother poked her with her foot. "Are Mr. Stuart's engineers so hopeless that you can't render an opinion?"

His blue eyes burned when they looked at her. She could feel their heat.

Only when he looked away was she able to respond. "They're, well, they can learn, but I don't know what will happen outside the structure of the classroom. We need a rehearsal."

"Of course we do!" Pearl declared. "We'll plan every detail of the Japanese visit. Then Maggie will concentrate her instruction on how your people should handle themselves in those situations."

"I already have a loose schedule..." Kyle indicated the papers he'd brought.

Pearl waved them away. "I mean *plan every detail*. Decide where to eat and what to eat. Plan the entertainment activities. We'll assemble the guest lists and give your people a small curriculum vitae about each person who'll attend so they can practice possible topics of conversation. Ruby, you'll have to make a note of that since Magnolia appears preoccupied."

Maggie only smiled. The Jewels exchanged looks.

"You mentioned a reception—have a dry run and discuss how everyone should behave," Pearl continued. "And for heaven's sake, don't take anything for granted. If you're planning a dinner, then have one ahead of time where you'll serve your staff the same food you'll serve the Japanese."

"Is all this necessary?" Kyle asked.

Three heads nodded vigorously. One smiled bemusedly.

Ruby waved a sheaf of papers. "Mr. Stuart, only something of vital importance would divert my energies from the unending struggle to alleviate the unbalanced burden women bear in our society."

"It's just like when we prepared for Maggie's debut," Opal said. "You should have seen her dress. It was white," she said dreamily. "With yards and yards of net holding out the skirt."

"Opal, let's not bore Mr. Stuart with the details of Magnolia's underskirt. The point Opal is attempting to make is that we practiced for weeks with Magnolia. We had small luncheons and teas where she could get acquainted with the other girls. By the night of the ball, she and her friends were seasoned young ladies."

Kyle sent a questioning glance at her and Maggie had to agree. His staff needed the experience.

"What if something comes up that hasn't been rehearsed?" he asked.

"There's no way we can anticipate every incident that will occur, but if Magnolia has been instructing your staff correctly, they'll be able to acquit themselves nicely."

Kyle capitulated, as Maggie had known he would.

She, herself, had found that it was simply easier to give in to overpowering forces these days, and the Jewels were only one of those forces.

The other made itself known as she walked Kyle onto the porch.

The screen door had barely banged shut behind them when Maggie flung herself into Kyle's arms. He staggered backward.

"Maggie," he gasped when he came up for air. "Those lace curtains aren't opaque."

"Don't care." She stood on tiptoe and nipped his earlobe. "You have cute ears."

"Mag—" Breath hissing between his teeth, Kyle sat heavily in the swing.

Maggie sat beside him and kissed his other ear.

"This is going to be the longest night of my life. Do we have to wait until tomorrow?" he asked.

As she toyed with the buttons on his shirt—and darned if they didn't just slip right through the buttonholes—Maggie tried to think why they were waiting until tomorrow. What a stupid idea. "Why wait?"

"Yeah, I was thinking the same thing. Can you get away tonight?" Kyle whispered against the side of her neck.

Maggie shivered. "It'll be forever. They'll be awake for hours." She ran her fingers across his chest.

"I'll buy you a ladder." He kissed her. "Climb down the tree."

There was something wrong with that plan. Maggie lifted her lips away from his to concentrate. "The hardware store is closed."

"*I'll drive into Atlanta.*" Kyle gripped her shoulders, his hands hot against her thin silk blouse.

"You can't fit a ladder in your car."

"Trust me, I'll find a way!"

Maggie believed him, but before she could tell him

so, the click of high-heeled shoes against polished wood sounded through the open window.

"Maggie? Are you still out there?"

"Yes, Aunt Opal."

"Is Mr. Stuart with you?"

She and Kyle looked at each other. Sanity returned. With a crooked smile, he started buttoning his shirt.

"He was just leaving," Maggie said regretfully.

"I'm going to turn on the porch light so he can see his way down the steps."

Kyle did a credible job of buttoning most of his shirt by the time the porch light flashed.

"Tomorrow," he promised before bounding down the steps.

"Yo, Mags!" Mitchell McCormick came up to her after Maggie's third and final seminar for the day.

"Not Mags, Mitch."

"Whatever. Here." He handed her a computer diskette. "I downloaded some stuff off the Internet. Thought you might be interested."

"That was sweet of you, Mitch." Maggie meant it. "But I don't have a computer."

"You don't have a computer?" He sounded as though she'd announced that she didn't have a head. "Everybody has a computer."

"I had one when I worked in Atlanta, but it belonged to the company."

"Was it one of ours?"

She laughed. "I don't know. It was just an ordinary computer."

Mitch looked pained. "Probably wasn't ours, then. Ours aren't ordinary."

"I could use a computer, though. Is there an extra one around here? Maybe a desk, too? It would be more convenient if I could leave some of my materials here instead of lugging them back and forth every night."

"I'll find you a computer." Mitch spoke as though he was about to embark on a life-or-death mission. "Talk to Janet. She'll find someplace to put you."

"I will. Thanks."

But not this afternoon. This afternoon, Maggie Jefferson was going shopping, and she wasn't going to feel the slightest bit guilty about spending the money.

Nevertheless, when she arrived home at four-thirty, she was glad that the Jewels weren't still in the back parlor at tea and able to see the packages in her arms.

That was unusual and Maggie felt a few qualms about being so late. They must have already finished and were in the kitchen preparing dinner.

Dinner. He was going to cook for her. She sighed. Kyle was picking her up at six and she wanted plenty of time to get ready.

Maggie had just cut the tags off her purchases when there was a soft but firm I-know-you're-in-there knock at her door.

"Maggie?" It was her mother.

As the knob turned, Maggie pushed several bits of lace and silk beneath the new skirt she'd bought. "Yes, Mama?"

Ruby shut the door behind her. She cleared her

throat. "You're going out with Mr. Stuart tonight, Magnolia?"

Her mother *never* called her Magnolia.

"Yes, ma'am."

She knew. Somehow, her mother knew.

"He's the one, isn't he?"

Maggie swallowed. "This is only our first date."

Ruby, arms crossed, leaned against the door. "Doesn't matter. I don't believe I even went on a date with your father."

Maggie found it unsettling to realize that she understood perfectly.

"Those were the days of free love and demonstrations against the draft. I met him at a rally. He'd just graduated, and had lost his student deferment. He said his name was Buddy. It probably wasn't his real name, but I never knew any other."

Ruby, her face softened with memories, rested her gaze on Maggie. "We talked and talked."

Maggie sat on the edge of her bed. Her mother had never voluntarily discussed Maggie's father and Maggie had long ago ceased trying to pry information out of her. She only knew that he was from the North and Ruby hadn't been able to find his family.

"At the rally, there were several recent graduates in the same situation, and it looked like they'd get drafted. At that time, the government still offered exemptions to married men and so several of us decided to marry them."

"Just like that?"

"Oh, I already knew I wanted to marry Buddy. And

I had to do something. I couldn't just let him go off to war." She shook her head. "The next evening, we were married in a group ceremony under the stars by the Church of Celestial Light."

"It sounds beautiful."

Ruby smiled. "We had to join the church and were given star names. That's why I never learned his real name. I don't even have a picture of him. He had blue eyes though."

Maggie felt a jolt. "Well, what happened?"

Ruby's face became hard again. "The Church of Celestial Light wasn't recognized by the government and he was drafted anyway. I never saw him again."

"Oh, Mama."

Ruby shrugged. "But I didn't mean to talk about all that. I want to talk about you."

"What about me?" Maggie asked warily.

Ruby walked toward her, withdrawing pamphlets from beneath her shawl. "It's been a while since we've had a woman-to-woman talk."

Maggie shifted uncomfortably. "Mama, I'm twenty-eight years old."

"And I was on the Pill," Ruby said with a significant look. "It didn't matter. There's something that happens to Jefferson women when they fall in love," she continued. "I thought I was immune, but I wasn't. Anyway, it's a different world out there now, and I want you to be careful." She handed Maggie the pamphlets.

Feeling incredibly awkward, Maggie accepted them.

"Promise me you'll read those before you leave."

"But there are a lot of them here!" Maggie protested.

"Magnolia, promise me."

Maggie nodded.

"I also bought these for you—not that they'll do any good, but you might as well try." Ruby held out a box of condoms. "They're latex and have the highest safety rating. Never use lambskin."

"Thank you, Mama," Maggie said in a strangled voice. She decided against telling her mother that she'd bought her own this afternoon.

"Well." As she had the other night, Ruby touched Maggie's cheek. "He seems like a good man—for a Yankee," she said, and quietly left the room.

A variety of emotions bombarded Maggie. *There's something that happens to Jefferson women when they fall in love.* And howdy.

Maggie was reading the pamphlets—talk about mood killers—when there was a furtive knocking at her door.

"Maggie, dear?"

"Yes, Aunt Opal?" Maggie shoved the condoms under her bed and the pamphlets under her new skirt. But the new underwear was already under there, so she had to shove the pamphlets under the stretchy top she'd bought, where they made odd squarish lumps.

Carrying a brown cardboard box, Opal tiptoed into the room. "This is so romantic. As soon as I saw that you had the glow, I ordered these." She giggled. "You were glowing so much, I had them shipped express."

Opal moved the stretchy top and revealed the pamphlets.

Maggie's heart stopped.

"Oh, good, your mother's already been by." Opal brushed the pamphlets aside and plopped herself on the bed next to Maggie. "Look what I brought you." She opened the box and dumped the contents onto the feminist quilt. "I ordered them from the back of *Soap Bubbles* magazine."

Condoms of every shape, size, color and style gleamed up at them.

"I specified extra-large," Maggie's great-aunt informed her, then added in a whisper, "But I really think they're all the same size. The extra-large on the package probably refers to men's egos." She tittered and poked her elbow in Maggie's ribs.

Maggie was speechless. Utterly speechless.

"Just look at all these." Opal admired the display. "So many more choices than we had in my day. Not that they did any good, but you still should make the effort."

"Well, I—I—"

"Oh, Maggie, you must." Opal patted her knee. "I realize some men can be so unpleasant about the subject, but you must remain firm—they certainly will." She clapped her hand over her mouth and giggled again. "I'm being so naughty, but really—" she held up a pack of four in neon green, blue, pink and orange "—how can one be serious when faced with these?"

"I have no idea," Maggie managed to say.

Opal paddled through the foil sea on Maggie's bed. "They've even got flavored ones."

"Really?" Maggie asked faintly.

"Oh, yes," Opal confirmed with a vigorous nod. She tossed four packets at Maggie. One was empty.

"Oh!" Opal blushed and snatched it back. "They said it was tangerine and I thought, why tangerine and not plain orange? Does it really taste like tangerine? So I opened it. I didn't think you'd mind, unless tangerine is a particular favorite of yours?"

Maggie shook her head.

"Oh, good. Well, it smelled like plain orange and frankly, any nuances of flavor were lost—"

"That's okay. There are plenty more here." Maggie picked up a strip of animal-print condoms. "Lions, and tigers, and bears. Oh, my."

"Perhaps not on the first date, dear," Opal gently suggested.

Maggie dropped them back into the box. "Aunt Opal, I hardly know what to say. This is so... thoughtful of you. Thanks."

"Oh, Maggie." Opal sighed. "I remember what it was like when I first met Coral's papa." Opal gazed off into space, the same look on her face that had been on Ruby's. "He had the most beautiful blue eyes."

Maggie, who had been studying the startling array of condoms, stared at her aunt.

"He was selling brushes and came to our door. It was such a hot day and I gave him a glass of iced tea. We sat on the swing and talked." She smiled. "Then I went with him on his calls. He sold ever so many more brushes when I was with him." Opal dimpled, then her smile faded. "But I was a Jefferson and Aunt Beryl couldn't get over the fact that he was a Yankee salesman." Opal tilted her chin. "So I ran away with him. At first it was fun and romantic, but after a while, I wanted a place of our own, especially once Coral was on the way. I came back here, and he was going to send for me when he had enough money saved up."

And he never had, Maggie knew.

"Well." Opal patted Maggie's knee and stood. "Love is wonderful, Maggie. I don't regret a minute and you mustn't, either." She smiled. "I'll let you finish getting ready now."

Maggie surveyed the assortment of condoms. *I'll never be ready for some of these.*

After the two visits, Maggie was rushed. She'd finished her bath and had put on her new pink underwear, which managed to be sweet and sexy at the same time, when there was a no-nonsense knock at her door.

"Magnolia?"

Her *grandmother*.

Maggie dived for her robe as the doorknob turned. Opal's condoms were still spread all over the bed. Maggie ran and sat in the middle of the packets, spreading her robe over as many as she could.

"Magnolia? Good, you haven't left yet. I was afraid I wouldn't arrive back in time." A breathless Pearl, dressed in her going-out clothes and clutching her purse to her ample bosom, closed the door behind her. "It has come to my attention that you are stepping out with Mr. Stuart."

"He's asked me to dinner, yes."

Pearl eyed her. "Lately, you have had a look about you. One that I have seen on two other occasions. One that I...that I may have even had myself." She advanced toward the bed.

Maggie cringed, the edges of dozens of packets digging through the satin robe and her new underwear. Out of the corner of her eye, neon glowed and foil gleamed. She could practically hear the animal prints growling. Oh, well. Her grandmother probably wouldn't even know what these were.

"It has..." Pearl's gaze swept the bed. "Opal and your mother have spoken to you, I see."

"Yes." Maggie's voice sounded high and strained.

"I hope you listened, Magnolia. The women in our family tend toward the 'grand passion.'" She gazed off into the distance. "Once we love, we love with our whole beings. Perhaps too much. The men...the men have failed to understand the depths of our devotion." She turned her gaze on Maggie. "I remember the first time I saw your grandfather. I was serving doughnuts to our dear soldiers at the USO. He was from the North—"

"A Yankee, Grandmother?" Maggie couldn't resist.

"It didn't seem important at the time." She smiled. "We were married on a Saturday and he shipped out that Monday." She sighed. You can't tell from the black-and-white wedding picture, but he had the most beautiful blue eyes."

A Yankee with blue eyes. There was a trend here.

"I wrote to him, but his letters stopped coming. I don't know if he ever got the one telling him about your mother. Well." Pearl dug in her purse and withdrew a box of plain, ordinary condoms. "These are for you, not that I believe they'll do any good. Somehow, we Jefferson women are destined to bear the child of our one, true love. Your goal, Magnolia, should be to bear that child when you're certain her father will be around to help raise her."

"Thank you," Maggie managed to say, setting the box beside her and trying to cover up more of Opal's exotic offerings.

"I bought them in Atlanta to spare your reputation," Pearl announced, and with a curt nod, left the room.

Her grandmother had just driven all the way to Atlanta to avoid buying condoms at the Jeffersonville Drug Emporium. Maggie, grappling with a variety of emotions, abandoned her tiny evening purse in favor of a larger bag, into which she put a sentimental sampling from each box.

Then she finished getting ready for her date with a blue-eyed Yankee.

8

ALL THREE JEWELS answered the door when Kyle arrived at the Jefferson home. For a moment, he thought they meant to prevent Maggie from leaving.

"Good evening, Mr. Stuart."

"Good evening, Mrs. Jefferson...Ms. Jefferson...Miss Opal."

She giggled. "Why, Mr. Stuart. You look so handsome in that blue sweater. I swear, my heart's all aflutter."

"Sounds like it's time to up the dose of your blood pressure medicine, Aunt Opal," Maggie's mother muttered.

Hurried footsteps sounded and they all turned to watch as Maggie galloped down the stairs.

Halfway down, she saw them and immediately modified her pace, descending the rest of the stairs sedately.

Kyle's mouth went dry and he expected one of the women to order her back upstairs to change out of the finest black skirt he'd ever seen. He glanced toward the women. Didn't they notice how long it made Maggie's legs look?

Kyle started to sweat, convinced that the three women could read his mind.

Maggie arrived at his side, smelling all sweet and fresh, but looking hot and bothered. Her cheeks were pink as she smiled first at him, then at the Jewels.

"Magnolia, please turn out the porch light when you arrive back home." Pearl looked Kyle right in the eye when she spoke.

Message received. "I won't keep her out too late."

"Oh, but don't rush your evening," Opal said. "I'm sure we'll all be asleep when you get back, Maggie."

"But we're light sleepers," Ruby added, with another look at Kyle.

Maggie swung her purse over her shoulder and took his arm. "Ready?"

Kyle, feeling like a despoiler of young maidens, opened the door for her.

"Do you get that kind of send-off every time you go out on a date?" he asked once they were out of earshot.

"It was worse when I was in school. They'd interrogate any boy brave enough to ask me out. Not many were."

Laughing, Kyle opened the car door. "I've already been questioned."

"So you have." She swung those legs of hers into his car.

Kyle needed a few moments to regain his equilibrium. "I don't mind," he told her, and started the car. "I know they're only doing it because they care about you."

"And I care about them. Otherwise, I wouldn't have moved back home."

It must be frustrating for her to have returned to

such a restrictive life-style after being on her own, Kyle thought. "You're a very special woman, Maggie."

"Because I care about my family? What kind of a woman would I be if I didn't?"

One he wouldn't like as much, Kyle acknowledged. "It's the way you care about them. Like climbing out your window rather than openly defying your grandmother."

He felt Maggie look at him. "And who checked us out to make sure we wouldn't insult his friend?"

"That was different."

"I don't think so." She looked at him in a way that made him feel she was giving him undeserved credit.

He gave a short laugh. "Well, I hope they don't give you too much trouble about going out with me tonight, because I intend this night to be the first of many."

At that Maggie started laughing. When he looked questioningly at her, she only laughed harder. "They're way ahead of you on that one."

THEY TOOK A SPECIAL elevator up to the penthouse and Maggie was charmed to detect signs of nervousness in Kyle. He opened the door and she heard him expel a long breath.

"Home sweet home," he said, and waited for her reaction.

"It's nice," she said, looking around. "Very you." The penthouse was decorated in a modern, masculine low-maintenance sort of way, heavy on the electronics. He'd made an effort—there weren't basketball hoops or neon beer signs. But the best thing about it was that

Maggie could tell a woman hadn't lived here before. Except for the vase of mixed flowers on the glass dining table, the entire place was devoid of feminine touches.

"It's probably not your style." There was an appealing uncertainty in his voice.

Maggie slung her bulky purse onto a black leather couch. "It's *exactly* the way I'd hoped it would look."

He grinned, his teeth gleaming, and just stared at her for a moment.

The unguarded longing Maggie saw in his eyes fueled her own yearning. The tension that was always between them hummed to life. She could feel her body pulling toward him. Or was that leaping?

She should probably keep her purse close by.

Aware of herself and her body in a way she hadn't been with any other man, Maggie walked across the room, not intending to stop until she was in Kyle's arms. To heck with dinner. She didn't want to wait any longer.

Warmed by desire, the joints and tendons of her body became looser and her walk turned into the prowl of a jungle cat stalking its mate.

Maybe she should have brought those animal-print condoms, after all.

SLOW DOWN, TIGER.

He had to stop projecting his fantasies onto Maggie. She was only walking across the room and he was ready to grab her and haul her off to his lair.

There was plenty of time for grabbing and hauling

later. He'd promised her dinner. That look in her eyes was probably hunger.

Kyle dragged his gaze away from her and gestured toward the kitchen bar. "Would you like a glass of wine?"

She blinked several times and he wondered if she'd heard him—or if he'd spoken coherently. He certainly wasn't *thinking* coherently. "Wine?" he repeated, enunciating clearly.

"Yes." She sort of flowed onto the bar stool.

Swallowing, Kyle managed to get to the kitchen on the other side without touching her. When he withdrew a wine bottle from the refrigerator, he banged it against the shelf. Ditto with the wineglasses, which clanked when he removed them from their wooden holder. At this rate, he might not make it though dinner with all his crockery intact.

Then he made the mistake of making eye contact with her. At this rate, they might not make it through dinner at all.

THE JUMPIER HE WAS, the better Maggie liked it. The idea that Kyle hadn't entertained many women was infinitely appealing. She felt inexplicably territorial with Kyle and found herself thinking of things that had never occurred to her before—like wanting to sit in the leather sofa long enough for it to absorb her perfume and remind Kyle of her after she left, as well as to warn off any other women. Especially to warn off any other women.

He set the glasses on the counter and poured her wine without spilling any, to his visible relief.

Maggie smothered her smile by sipping her wine. "What's for dinner? I don't smell anything cooking."

"Oh, dinner." He laughed and stuck his hands in his back pockets. "I'm just a beginner cook. I thought I'd broil some steaks and bake potatoes in the microwave."

"Sounds great." Man the hunter, bringing meat for his mate.

He gave her a wary look. "You're not going to watch me, are you?"

Maggie leaned her elbows on the bar. "I find watching a man cook for me...exciting."

Kyle stared at her and licked his lips. "Okay." He looked around the kitchen, as if trying to figure out what he was doing there.

Maggie drank her wine and watched Kyle's endearing maneuvers in the kitchen.

He slapped two steaks on a pristine broiler pan and turned on the oven. Then he stuffed two of the largest potatoes Maggie had ever seen in her life into the microwave and set the timer for three minutes.

"They might take a little longer than that," she said.

"You think so?" he asked seriously.

Maggie nodded, feeling herself fall that much deeper in love with him. She wasn't sure when she first realized she loved him. It was as though the love had always existed and was waiting for something to trigger it. Feelings of love triggered by potatoes. Did she have it bad, or what? "Don't forget to pierce them first."

"Just getting around to that." With the tip of a paring knife, he made precise, evenly placed punctures in the skin of the potatoes.

Maggie could barely keep from vaulting over the bar and wrapping her arms around him. She drank her wine, instead.

"I've already made salads." Kyle got two bowls out of the refrigerator and carried them to the table.

Maggie swiveled on the bar stool to follow his progress.

He looked up and held her gaze. "We can eat the salads while the steak and potatoes cook," he offered.

"Okay." She slithered off the stool.

Kyle clenched and unclenched his fist.

Time didn't appear to be settling his nerves. She grabbed his wine from the bar and brought it with her. "Here you go." Her fingers brushed his.

He jerked and liquid splashed over his hand.

"Kyle, relax. You don't have to be nervous."

"I'm not nervous." He dabbed at his hand with a napkin.

"It's okay, really. I find it kind of flattering."

"It's not nerves." Closing his eyes, he inhaled. "It's just so damn difficult for me to keep from touching you. And once I touch you, I'm not going to want to stop."

Maggie set her wineglass down. "And why would I want you to stop?"

"Because it's just not cool to grab a woman the instant you get her into your home."

"I don't feel cool," she said, and lifted her arms.

Kyle's were around her before she touched his shoulders.

"Oh, Maggie," he breathed, holding her tight. "I've imagined you here for so long that I can't believe you *are* here."

As her mouth settled against his, Maggie felt an inevitable rightness. Kyle was the one. The only one. The right one.

The right one raised his head and sniffed. "What's that smell? Are the steaks burning?"

"Burning meat doesn't smell like that."

They both noticed the smoke at the same time. Kyle ran toward the kitchen and pulled open the oven.

Smoke rolled out.

The stench was horrible. He took out the broiler pan, but the steaks weren't yet browned.

Smoke continued to come from inside the oven. Kyle turned it off and Maggie flipped on the exhaust fan.

When the smoke cleared, Kyle peered inside, then shut the door, a sheepish expression on his face.

"What is it?"

He pulled Maggie out of the kitchen and over to the French doors, which opened onto a tiny terrace. "I, ah, have never used the oven before."

"Never?" Maggie was incredulous. "You've lived here for what...six years?"

He nodded. "That was the foam packing material around the burners."

Maggie brought her fingers to her mouth, but couldn't hold back the laughter. "You really don't cook, do you?"

"No," he admitted. "But I wanted to for you."

"Oh, Kyle." Maggie sighed and leaned against the terrace railing.

Kyle leaned next to her. "We can go out, if you'd like."

All Jeffersonville was at their feet while she was here with Kyle, away from prying eyes. "No way. Once the smoke clears, you can pan-fry those steaks in some cracked pepper and wine. They'll be great. You've used the burners before?"

"Mostly to heat soup," he confessed, then grimaced. "I'm sorry, Maggie. This evening was supposed to be special."

"It *is* special. We're together—and alone. That's plenty to celebrate—and weren't we celebrating?"

His gaze swept over her. "We'd just started, as I recall."

At that instant, Maggie knew dinner was a long, long time away. She leaned toward him and ran her fingers over the soft, cotton sweater that neatly defined his trim torso. Her fingertips were so sensitized, she could feel each individual thread. "I'm having trouble remembering...refresh my memory?"

Kyle captured her wandering fingers and held them over his heart. Maggie could feel the thudding.

He said nothing—he didn't need to, or rather his eyes said it all for him. He wanted her and he wanted her now.

Maggie let herself become lost in those eyes. She found the intense blue warming rather than cooling.

Then Kyle bent his head and kissed her hand. Lacing her fingers through his, he drew her back into the penthouse. As they walked by the leather sofa, Maggie snagged her purse.

SIMPLY TOUCHING HER hand was almost more than Kyle could bear. He actually felt light-headed just walking into the bedroom.

In order to regain control, he started calculating square roots in his head. Nine was too easy. Twelve...three point four six four one...

He reached the door of his bedroom. Why hadn't he noticed that his bed looked so weird before? It and the control-panel headboard he'd designed dominated the room. The whole thing looked like an electronic sleep-testing facility.

No amount of candles—and he'd bought a dozen of them—would make this place look romantic. He was going to have to light them anyway and hope the vanilla scent would mask the smell of burnt plastic and foam.

He opened the nightstand drawer for some matches, but it caught on something. Kyle pulled harder, and just as the drawer slid all the way out and landed on the floor, he remembered that he'd generously stocked it with condoms that afternoon.

They spilled out in a foil puddle right at Maggie's feet.

Real smooth, Stuart. He'd just committed a serious

breach of condom etiquette. A guy could have one with him when he went out, but not two. One was for serendipity, two raised the question of unwelcome expectations.

Now, a nightstand was different, but here, too, numbers sent a critical message. Three was the right number. Three meant prepared, but not pushy. Three meant "stay the night, if you want." With three, a guy could casually say, "Let me check the medicine cabinet. I might be able to find some in there," if the situation warranted. Three was cool and classy. Modern.

But an entire drawer stuffed full sent a message Kyle didn't even want to think about. Why hadn't he immediately stored the extras in the bathroom?

"Gee, I think you've managed to find a couple of brands I don't have," Maggie said, poking through the pile with her foot.

"What?"

Silently, she opened her purse and turned it upside down.

A condom waterfall splashed into the pool at her feet.

They both stared at it. A couple of the fluorescent ones glowed dimly, like plankton in the ocean.

There was a message there, Kyle supposed. Maybe if he stared long enough, the packets would rearrange themselves into letters.

"I suppose this would be the time to explain about my family's blue-eyed-Yankee fertility curse," Maggie said.

He had blue eyes. He'd been born in the North. "Fertility curse?"

She gestured to the floor and they both stooped and gathered the condoms. Maggie tossed hers into the drawer with his, Kyle noticed, feeling cheered.

"I've been told that my father and grandfather were blue-eyed Yankees. Opal fell for one, too."

"Is that bad?" Kyle asked. He could always get colored contact lenses.

"Apparently, always fruitful." She stood. "I was given those to try to break with tradition."

"By whom?" Kyle fit the drawer back on the runners.

"The fancy ones are from Opal, my mother and grandmother gave me the others."

So everybody had known what was on the agenda tonight. No wonder they'd subjected him to those strange looks. Kyle felt a case of performance anxiety coming on.

He found the matches and carefully pushed the drawer closed. "They're, ah, more liberal than I'd supposed."

"Just practical, I think."

The mood was slipping away. He had to do something. Striking a match, he lit the cluster of candles on his nightstand then glanced at Maggie.

She was staring at the ceiling. "Is that...a mirror?"

"Skylight." Kyle pressed a square on the headboard panel and the dark covering in the ceiling slid away, revealing the night sky. Then he turned off the room light.

She gasped softly.

Shadows from the candle flames danced along the edges of the room. Stars twinkled down at them.

"That's the most romantic thing I've ever seen."

"You think so?"

"And the candles..." She sighed. "Everything is perfect."

Desire and relief—but primarily desire—rushed through him. "Not quite," he said, his voice strained.

The next instant she was in his arms, warm and soft, her perfume mixing with the scent of vanilla from the candles. When he nuzzled the side of her neck, he almost couldn't smell the burnt plastic. "Now it's perfect."

She laughed and echoed his words. "Not quite." And she raised her mouth.

Kyle meant to savor this kiss, since all their others had been interrupted. He wanted memories of a complete kiss, from the getting-settled part, through the exploring part to the finish, when they'd breathe together and their lips would tingle.

He wanted to be able to relive each moment when Maggie wasn't with him.

But he made a mistake—a tiny miscalculation. He'd thought he'd still be able to think once Maggie touched him.

He couldn't.

She ran her hands under his sweater and the next thing he knew, he'd pulled it off along with the T-shirt beneath it.

He saw the candlelight reflected in her eyes as she

studied him. The small smile of pleasure at what she saw tweaked his male pride.

Maggie ran her hands over his chest and shoulders and he closed his eyes, mindlessly enjoying the sensation. Then she stood on tiptoe and kissed his throat and jaw.

"Oh, Maggie..." His voice didn't sound like his own.

He was fast losing control. He wasn't supposed to lose control—he was supposed to *be* in control. Burying his hands in her hair, he held her face still while he kissed her, skipping the getting-settled part and lingering in the exploring part. He never wanted to get to the ending part.

Sliding his hands down her back, he pulled her hips close to his and rocked against her.

Her moan vibrating against his lips jolted him back to awareness.

Clothes. Clothes were in the way and they didn't have to be.

His fingers found the zipper to her skirt and he tugged.

Nothing happened. Or rather something happened, but it wasn't what he expected.

Maggie pushed herself out of his arms and unzipped her skirt, kicking off her shoes and wiggling her hips until the skirt fell down around her ankles.

She kicked it, too.

Kyle's knees gave way and he sat heavily on the bed.

This brought his face about even with the end of Maggie's top.

His hands had an embarrassing quiver to them as he peeled the stretchy fabric up and over her head.

Her skin looked like lace in the candlelight. No, wait, that *was* lace—lace the color of her skin. Lace lovingly molding curves and hollows he longed to explore.

Kyle stared, not moving. If he moved even a fraction of an inch, it was all over.

If *she* moved a fraction of an inch, it was all over.

"You're so beautiful," he whispered.

"Aren't you going to touch me?" she asked.

"No!" He swallowed and clenched his hands. "Not for a minute or two." Square root of two...one point four one four...

She stepped forward and his breathing picked up.

Then she knelt and he thought he'd have a heart attack, but she was just taking off his shoes and socks.

Her hair brushed his legs and feet.

Kyle sat on his hands and calculated furiously. Square root of...twenty. "Four point four..."

"What did you say?"

He gave a short laugh. "Actually, I think it was 'four point four.' It's not important."

She looked puzzled.

"I just want you so much," he explained simply. "And I want you to want me just as much."

Her fingers worked at his belt. "I do."

He doubted it. No human could want another as much as he wanted this woman. Maggie.

Tenderness, desire and an urge to possess her bombarded him all at once.

Standing, he held out his hand to help her up, then quickly finished undressing.

HE WAS GOLDEN in the candlelight.

And he wanted her so very much.

But then, she wanted him, too.

Kyle drew back the sheets, picked Maggie up and set her in his bed.

The touch of his hands ignited the heat she always felt when she was near him, and this time she wouldn't have to quench it suddenly. She could let it build to a white-hot intensity, then die gradually to glowing embers until the next time Kyle fanned it to flame.

He stretched out beside her, propping himself on an elbow. "This is very pretty," he said, his voice like sandpaper. With a finger, he lazily traced the edge of the expensive lace bra she'd bought this afternoon.

Maggie's skin tightened into goose bumps as she felt both hot and cold at the same time.

"Very pretty," he whispered. "But I think it's served its purpose, don't you?"

His questing finger found the hook hidden behind a tiny satin bow. With a gentle tug, it sprang free.

Maggie's mouth went dry as he peeled the lace away.

"Oh, Maggie."

He gazed at her with such wonder and awe that Maggie felt she was the most beautiful and desirable woman in the world. "Touch me," she whispered.

And for an instant, his hands cupped her breasts, replacing the lace, then he inhaled sharply. He closed his eyes, his lips moving silently, then reached out and gathered her in his arms, rolling until she was on top of him.

Starting at her neck, he ran his hands down her back in long strokes, catching and sweeping away her underwear.

"Oh, Maggie." It seemed to be all he could say, but it was enough. She understood.

Then he drew her down to him and captured her mouth in a searing kiss.

The fire was building too fast. Maggie broke the kiss and, sighing against his mouth, spread her hands over his chest. He had hair on his chest. Dense, springy, masculine hair. She kissed her way down to it and inhaled. Kyle clutched at her shoulders.

"Five point four," he groaned.

"What?"

"Square roots...I'm calculating square roots."

"Why?"

"Because you're driving me insane, that's why!"

"Well, maybe you should try driving *me* insane..."

He flipped her over, quickly and efficiently, before she could guess that he was going to.

"Kyle—"

He trapped the rest of her words with his mouth as he caressed her with his hands.

And the temperature rose.

Maggie sensed an inevitability about their lovemaking, as though she'd been destined for Kyle. As though he'd been destined for her.

And then she stopped thinking.

Kyle's hands and mouth were everywhere, touching, stroking, kissing, until Maggie couldn't tell if she'd finally lost her mind, or only just found it.

"Kyle," she moaned, and he opened the nightstand drawer.

Overhead was the Georgia night sky and when Kyle returned moments later, the stars framed his face.

He laced his fingers through hers and held himself above her.

Their gazes locked as he moved into her. They both stopped breathing. *He feels it, too*, Maggie thought. She could see it in his eyes, his blue, blue eyes.

They fused together, bonded by her heat. She felt it spread outward, enveloping them both.

And then he started to move, still watching her.

Maggie's fire became an inferno, building with every gasping breath she took, until she couldn't breathe anymore and let the heat consume her.

A rippling deep within her spread outward, lapping at the flames until they cooled.

Maggie started breathing again in short panting gasps.

When she opened her eyes, she saw that Kyle was still watching her, his lips moving.

Just before he lowered his head and kissed her, Maggie distinctly heard, "Nine," and then he surged against her, shuddering almost instantly.

Maggie clasped him to her, feeling powerful and womanly and deeply satisfied.

"Oh, Maggie." He sighed, and nuzzled her neck.

She managed a shaky laugh. "What's this nine business? That was definitely a ten."

"Ten nothing. That was off the charts." He grazed a kiss across her jaw and raised his head. "I know this sounds like a line, but I swear it's never been like that for me before."

Of course not. Destiny didn't fool around.

Kyle moved away and reached for the bedding to wrap them in a cocoon.

Maggie turned to cuddle with him, then noticed a pale blue glow. "What's that?"

They both stared under the sheets, then Maggie started to laugh.

Kyle muttered under his breath. "I...just reached in the drawer. I didn't look...I'm sorry, Maggie, I—"

"Shh." Still laughing, Maggie put her fingers over his mouth. "It was the perfect choice. It matches your eyes."

9

MAGGIE SPENT the next several days in a haze of happiness. She intercepted the looks the Jewels gave her and each other, and she wanted to tell them that Kyle wasn't like the men they'd fallen in love with. He loved her. He wouldn't abandon her. He had a business here. A home. Roots.

One day, Maggie arrived home after her seminars to find boxes, plastic bags and foam packing material littering the foyer.

"Mama?" Maggie called, smiling at the Stuart Computers logo she found everywhere.

"Hey, Mags, we're in here."

Uh-oh. "Mitch?"

"Yeah."

Cautiously, Maggie wandered into the front parlor, which had apparently been converted into an office. She'd never mentioned Kyle's deception to her family and she doubted Kyle had told Mitch. "What's all this?"

"A computer," her mother answered. "Mr. McCormick has graciously been setting it up for us. This visit with the Japanese has strained Aunt Opal's index-card system. She and your grandmother used to carry a lot of plans in their heads anyway, and they're just not as young as they once were." Ruby flipped a switch and a full-color monitor sprang to life.

Mitch backed out from beneath an antique writing desk. "Hey, Ms. J., will you plug in the printer cord for me?" He pointed.

Ruby reached under a lamp table and plugged in another of what looked like dozens of electrical cords.

Maggie wondered if the electrical wiring in the old house was up to powering what was undoubtedly a state-of-the-art system. "Do you know anything about computers, Mama?"

"I've run into them from time to time," Ruby said. "But Mr. McCormick has promised to teach me the basics."

"Nothing much to it," Mitch said. "These days everything is point and click." His voice held the disgust of a computer pro for operating-system shells.

Ruby was already pointing and clicking.

"Does Opal know you're not planning to use her index cards?" Maggie asked.

"Oh, I'll use them," Ruby replied, holding up the familiar wooden box. "They'll be entered in my database." She started tapping on the keyboard. "Why, look! It says all I have to do is type in the names and addresses. There's even a space for Opal's notes."

"If you get into trouble, there's a tutorial." Mitch showed Ruby where it was.

"*Thank* you, Mr. McCormick."

Maggie was wondering how she would be able to apprise her two older relatives of Ruby's foray into advanced technology, when Opal called from the drawing room. "Ruby?"

"Aunt Opal," Maggie began.

"Hello, Maggie." Smiling, Opal sailed by. "Is my printout ready yet?"

Maggie felt as if she could use a good strong glass of tea. Only the Jewels appeared to have skipped afternoon tea today.

"Not yet," Ruby answered Opal. "Mr. McCormick needed an extension cable for the printer."

Mr. McCormick was eating a cookie.

Opal picked up the plate and an empty glass. "No more lemon cookies for you, Mr. McCormick." She dimpled at him. "You'll spoil your supper."

Maggie was adjusting to the fact that Mitchell McCormick appeared to have successfully befriended her family, when the doorbell rang.

"I'll get that," warbled Pearl from somewhere within the house.

"It'll be the pizza guy," Mitch announced, and hurdled the packing material as he raced Maggie's grandmother to the door.

To Maggie's astonishment, Pearl opened the door to a pizza delivery boy.

"Let me." Mitch paid him as Pearl accepted a huge box.

"Dinner in five minutes," she announced, then disappeared with the box.

Maggie followed her grandmother. "You're having pizza for dinner?"

"Yes. So convenient. I've told Jamison that the club

should offer such a lovely service, but he wouldn't hear of it." Pearl sniffed as she transferred the pizza onto a platter. "Mr. McCormick expressed his fondness for this particular establishment."

"I thought you liked to cook!" Maggie said.

"Yes, but we're very busy these days, Magnolia. Have you forgotten that we promised Mr. Stuart a preliminary schedule for the visit by this Friday?"

Maggie shook her head. The upcoming visit was uppermost in everyone's mind.

"I'm assuming that you're having dinner with Mr. Stuart again this evening."

"Um, yes."

"Well, you run along then. We've asked Mr. McCormick to dine with us. He's such a nice young man."

The world had turned upside down, Maggie was certain of it.

"We didn't recognize him at first, though," Pearl added, just as Maggie started to leave the room. "That first day, I particularly made note of his fine blue eyes." She smiled at Maggie. "Today, they appear to be brown."

"THEY'RE PUNISHING ME for the Mitch thing, aren't they?" It was Friday night, and Kyle and Maggie were eating pizza for dinner. He'd just looked at another in an unending set of printouts from Jefferson Protocol Consultants. Who'd given those women access to a laser printer, anyway?

Maggie picked off the green olives on her slice of pizza and transferred them to Kyle's. "They obviously know about it, but they've met the real Mitch and they like him. He's teaching Mama about the computer."

Kyle indicated the papers. "She learns fast." He picked up Thursday's preliminary schedule and studied it as he bit into his olive-heavy slice. He could take or leave the olives, but Maggie didn't like wasting them and he liked pleasing her. Really liked it.

"We thought sending someone to meet Mr. Matsuzaka and his party at the Atlanta airport would be a nice touch," Maggie ventured when Kyle remained silent. "We'll charter a bus to bring them here."

"I see you have them staying at the Jeffersonville Inn," he commented.

"It's the only place to stay in Jeffersonville, other than Mrs. Monroe's bed-and-breakfast. And she only has the two rooms."

"I assumed they'd be staying at the Worthington by the airport." He glanced up at her.

"Why?"

This is where it got tricky. He didn't want to offend Maggie. "I've stayed at the Jeffersonville Inn. It's...quaint." And that had been years ago. No telling what had happened in the interim.

"Are you intimating that the Jeffersonville Inn is not good enough for the Japanese?"

"Uh...they're a sophisticated bunch."

Maggie eyed him. "The Jeffersonville Ladies' Auxiliary will be helping the MacGruders with the extra work and cooking, though Mrs. MacGruder will be making her baking-powder biscuits herself. I defy anyone to have one of Mrs. MacGruder's biscuits and not want to come back for more."

Oookay. The Jeffersonville Inn it was.

Maggie handed him Friday's schedule. "All the entertainment we have planned is in Jeffersonville. After all, this *is* where the Stuart building is."

He whistled long and low when he finished glancing at Friday and Saturday's schedules. What was with the Jewels? With all the tours and teas going on, something disastrous was bound to happen. He wanted something much simpler—and less risky. Fortunately, Sunday was only a farewell picnic brunch on the grounds of the Jeffersonville Baptist Church. The Japanese might like that. But he had to cut out some of this other stuff and he had to do it without offending Maggie and her relatives.

"The ladies of the church plan to send them off with boxes of fried chicken and potato salad for the trip back," Maggie told him.

"Ah..." Kyle puffed out a breath. "This is an ambitious schedule," he said at last. "I didn't have anything so elaborate in mind when I asked for your help."

"Neither did I, at first," she said. "But it makes sense. These people are coming halfway around the world to visit your company and others. They're looking for a place to live. You want them to feel welcome, don't you?"

"Yes, but..." He gestured to the papers she was sliding into her folder. "This is going overboard."

"Overboard? I don't think so. The Japanese talk about *keiretsu*, which I'm probably not pronouncing right. It means the company family. Jeffersonville is part of your company family."

She wasn't taking hints. "Oh, come on, Maggie, this visit is turning into a circus."

Her brown eyes registered hurt. "The Japanese want to get to know people. This is a far better way than your canned tour with a film at the end like the one I took this morning."

Kyle stared at her in surprise. "You took our tour?"

"Yes, and it was ugly."

"Hey, just let me worry about the tour. You stick to the town activities."

"I had Mitch and the others take me on the tour for a practice run." She shook her head. "You are sorely in need of some pizzazz."

He gave her a look. "That's not all I'm in need of." He tossed the pizza back into the box.

She willingly met his embrace.

Kyle rested his chin on the top of her head. "Oh, Maggie, if I didn't have these nights with you, I think I'd go crazy."

"I know." She sighed against his chest. "It's nuts at home. Grandmother has committee meetings scheduled from ten o'clock until suppertime. I don't think there's a citizen of Jeffersonville who isn't involved in this visit one way or another."

"Maggie?" He pulled her away from him until he could look into her eyes. "I want to wake up next to you in the morning. I want to see you all warm and soft from sleep. I want to hold you for hours." It was humbling to realize how necessary Maggie had become to him and how the few hours they spent with each other weren't enough anymore.

"Kyle..." She bit her lower lip.

"Stay all night with me tonight."

"I can't."

"Why not?"

She gave him a look.

Kyle knew it was because of the gossips. She was right. He knew she was right.

But he didn't like it. "Okay, but when this is all over, you and I are going to have a talk."

A TALK COULD ONLY MEAN one thing: Kyle wanted to take their relationship to the next level, and he surely knew that in the conservative community of Jeffersonville, the next level was marriage.

Maggie was already outside the bounds of propriety and the Jewels were looking the other way. They weren't about to turn their backs.

Maggie also knew that Kyle would never ask her to marry him if his company was in jeopardy. Therefore, she was going to do her best to see that it wasn't—even if it meant overseeing each detail of the Matsuzaka visit herself.

Which is precisely what she did for the next week, nearly driving herself insane in the process.

"Magnolia," called her grandmother as Maggie was getting ready to leave for the Stuart building. "Today, you must insist that Mr. Stuart find out exactly how many people we're to prepare for."

"All right, Grandmother." She ought to write a note

to herself, Maggie thought. There were too many things to remember.

"Maggie?" Aunt Opal waylaid her. "Now, we still don't know what time the plane departs on Sunday, so we don't know if the picnic will be brunch or lunch."

"I'll try to find out, Aunt Opal," Maggie promised, shifting her armload of manila envelopes and handouts for her class. *Brunch, lunch and number of people,* she repeated to herself.

She made it to the front door.

"Maggie!" Her mother waved from her office. "Here's a list of the available interpreters and their bids for the weekend. We ought to book at least one, though Kyle says everyone speaks English. What do you think?"

"Even if they do, I think we probably need someone just to prevent misunderstandings." Maggie lifted her chin and her mother slipped the paper under it.

"Yes," Opal commented. "I frequently find it confusing to speak English all day."

Maggie and her mother exchanged a look. Unfortunately, Opal's comment made perfect sense.

Not much else did. As the date of the visit approached, she spent less and less time with Kyle, when she needed him more and more. It had been an entire week since they'd had a penthouse dinner.

They hadn't even gotten around to the animal-print condoms yet, and she'd bought special leopard-print underwear just for the event.

As she drove down Main Street, Maggie noticed the

new welcoming banners draped across storefronts and the Oriental paper lanterns hung in windows.

The visit had better be a success or else.

Or else she was afraid her relationship with Kyle wouldn't survive.

Right now it was in a holding pattern, which Maggie understood. But what if the Japanese decided to use another computer company for their chip? Worries about his company's future would occupy all Kyle's time.

And what about *her* future? Maggie pulled the ancient Cadillac into the Stuart parking lot. Would she follow Kyle if he had to leave Jeffersonville? Would he ask her to? And what about the Jewels?

It was all too much to contemplate now. She couldn't do anything about what-ifs, but she could concentrate on making this visit a success. It was obvious that everything important to her depended on it.

"Ms. Jefferson, your messages," said the receptionist as Maggie tried to sneak past.

"Yoo-hoo, Maggie," sang Janet from the doorway, though Maggie had tiptoed into the conference room. "A Mr. Jamison at the Jeffersonville Country Club has been trying to reach you."

Maggie dumped her materials on the table. One pink message slip fluttered to the carpet. Janet swooped on it and handed it to Maggie.

"Thanks," a weary Maggie said.

"Oops, I hear my phone!" Janet hurried out the door. "It's probably another call for you!"

Maggie closed her eyes.

"Hey, Mags, how's it going?" A chipper Mitch bounced into the conference room.

"You're early," Maggie grumbled. She hated being called Mags. Mitch knew this, of course.

"So what's up today?" He poked through the pile of papers she'd dumped on the table.

"Business cards—presenting and receiving."

Mitch rolled his eyes. "Isn't anything simple with those people?"

Maggie handed him a pair of scissors and pointed to the boxes in the corner. "New bilingual business cards for you all."

"I don't *belieeeve* this," Mitch said, hacking open the boxes.

"Believe it. We've also got to practice the dinner, the reception and the tour. And have a clothing check." Maggie mumbled the last.

"Hold it." There was nothing wrong with Mitch's hearing. "You're going to put me in a monkey suit, aren't you?"

"Just for a little while."

"No way." Mitch stood and backed up. He bumped into several other engineers who had arrived for class. "She's gonna make us wear monkey suits," he announced.

The men groaned.

"Absolutely not," said one. "We've gone along with everything else, but we're drawing the line at this."

Not today. Don't argue with me today. She gazed out at a sea of stubborn faces. "We are planning a formal dance for Mr. Matsuzaka's last night in town."

They all began talking at once. "Who's idea was that?"

"I don't know how to dance."

"I'm *not* wearing a monkey suit."

A wave of fatigue engulfed Maggie. She sat down abruptly. "Quiet, please," she said.

No one heard her. "Quiet!" she demanded in a louder voice.

But they were also babbling louder, their complaints numerous and, in Maggie's opinion, petty. Didn't they realize yet how important these details were to the success of the visit?

"*Quiet!*" she yelled.

There was an immediate and stunned silence.

And then she walked out.

Astonishingly, it was Mitch who came after her.

"Mags," he called, and came striding across the conference room. "I'm sorry. I know I get on people's nerves a lot." His forehead wrinkled. "It's just that I've always been better with machines than with people. With machines, you know what to expect. With people, you don't."

"Well..." Maggie swallowed against a sudden queasiness. "Nevertheless, I shouldn't have yelled at you all and I'm sorry I did." She'd been embarrassingly emotional lately. The littlest things set her off. Must be the stress.

He shrugged. "It's okay. We'll dress up if we have to, but I gotta tell you, nobody knows how to dance."

Maggie assured him that she'd go over a few easy steps with the group, but inwardly, she felt panicked.

There was too much to do and not enough time. She

had to focus on the outcome. On Kyle. Once he got the new computer chip, there would be nothing standing between them and happily-ever-after.

AT LAST IT WAS the day before the Japanese arrived. Maggie was meeting Kyle for a practice tour. Mitch and the others supposedly had their little speeches all rehearsed.

She hoped Mitch would cooperate. She wasn't up to his juvenile antics today.

At precisely eight twenty-five, Maggie arrived at the software lab. The tour was to begin at eight-thirty.

No one was in sight. Not even Kyle.

Eight-thirty, eight thirty-five... She recognized Kyle's rich tenor at last.

He and Mitch appeared, strolling down the aisle between the workstations.

Maggie fumed. Now the entire day's schedule would be off. "You're almost ten minutes late!" she announced as soon as they were within earshot.

"Be with you in a minute, Maggie," Kyle said, barely acknowledging her as he stopped to speak with someone else.

"Yo, Mags!" Mitch called. "Doughnuts in the snack bar." He gestured with the remains of a glazed doughnut, then stuffed it into his mouth as he sat at his bank of computers.

"No, thank you," she snapped. "We don't have time." She glanced at her watch as others laughed and chatted on their very slow way to their stations.

Mitch licked his fingers. "Want me to get you one?"

"No!" Maggie recoiled at the thought. She raised her voice. "Kyle? Shall we get started?"

He sent an impatient glance her way. "In a minute, Maggie."

"Hey, Mags, lighten up." Mitch scooted across the floor in his wheeled chair.

"Don't call me Mags!" She wanted to strangle him. She wanted to scream. She wanted to take all the neatly printed schedules she held, throw them in the air and walk out.

"Maggie?" Kyle had called to her.

"Could we *please* begin the tour?" What was the matter with him?

"Maggie." He took her arm in a gentle grip. "We can wait a few minutes—"

"No, we can't!" She shook off his hand. "We're already behind schedule!" Her voice was shrill.

"It's only fifteen minutes. We'll make it up." His calm voice irritated her further.

"No! Punctuality is very important to the Japanese." Maggie fumbled with her papers. "If we need an extra fifteen minutes, then I should schedule it now. Of course, that means lunch will be later, too." The manila envelope emptied schedules onto the floor. Still talking, Maggie bent to scoop them up. "The chef at the club will be furious. This will make the third change. Jamison—I should call Jamison."

Kyle slowly, but firmly, relieved Maggie of her papers.

"Don't!" she protested when he tossed them on a metal shelf.

Mitch bent to tug one of the schedules from underneath his chair wheels. "Mags, chill out." The paper ripped.

"Don't call me that!" she snarled, seizing her paper.

"Maggie, I think we need a break, not more practicing," Kyle said, and glanced around the lab. "Why don't you go home and relax?"

Go home and relax. He thought she was hysterical. So she'd been a little emotional lately. Hadn't they all? "Kyle," she said, her voice carefully modulated, "we ought to run through the tour."

"Don't worry. Go home. Rest. Put your feet up. Tomorrow will be fine."

Everything would *not* be fine. Maggie could sense it.

Somebody would mess up.

The Japanese would be offended.

Kyle wouldn't get the computer chip.

Stuart Computers would go bankrupt.

Kyle would leave.

Half of Jeffersonville would lose their jobs and the other half would lose the businesses that depended on Stuart Computers.

People would move away. Schools would empty. Property values would decline. The place would become a ghost town.

She, Magnolia Blossom Jefferson, great-great-granddaughter of LaRue Jefferson, Jeffersonville's founder, would be responsible for Jeffersonville's demise.

And all because she got a tad bit emotional.

Well, under those circumstances, who wouldn't?

10

IT WAS A BEAUTIFUL, warm afternoon in early June. The smell of freshly mown grass scented the puffs of air that teased Maggie's hair.

Members of the Jeffersonville Junior League hovered in the shade cast by the awning of the Jeffersonville Inn. Trying to appear dignified was the mayor of Jeffersonville and members of the city council, as well as the president of the chamber of commerce.

Opal and Ruby drilled the LaRue Jefferson Elementary School pupils in bowing and flag-waving. Pearl kept a lookout from inside the inn.

The Japanese were late.

"What if the bus broke down?" Kyle asked as the Jeffersonville High School Marching Rebel Band launched into the theme from *Rocky* yet another time.

"Their flight was delayed," Maggie reminded him. Again.

She was calm for the first time in days. Weeks. She'd given this visit her all and, she had to admit as she scanned the crowd, her all was pretty good.

At that moment, two charter buses turned down Main Street. The Rebels squawked to a halt and prepared to start the fanfare, brass gleaming in the sun. The drum major raised his baton in the air.

Kyle took a deep breath and straightened his tie. "Well, Maggie," he said, and winked at her. "Here we go."

FRIDAY MORNING. Day Two. The tour. It was time for the tour.

And Maggie was no longer calm.

Yesterday, Mr. Matsuzaka had appeared overwhelmed at the magnitude of Jeffersonville's greeting. When she thought about it from his point of view, Maggie admitted that Jeffersonville's enthusiasm might appear to verge on the desperate. Or were the townspeople merely reflecting Maggie's own desperation?

Kyle had been right. She and the Jewels had planned too much. Why hadn't she listened to him?

Too late now.

She couldn't look at Mitch. She couldn't look at anyone. But she did look at the clock. Eight twenty-seven. The Japanese were here. In the Stuart building. She tried not to hyperventilate.

Clutching her briefcase with both hands, she stood, dry-mouthed, at the entrance to the software lab.

She swallowed. Nothing happened. There was nothing to swallow. Water. She needed some water.

But Kyle and the Japanese had arrived. She could hear them. Then, out of the corner of her eye, Maggie noticed something moving.

Mitch was waving to get her attention.

Oh, no, now what?

He pointed to his monitor. RELAX, it blinked.

Maggie's eyes widened, but just before the group came within sight of Mitch's station, he punched a key and the message disappeared.

Kyle didn't appear nervous in the least.

Maggie's heart thundered. She nodded to Mr. Matsuzaka, whom she'd met yesterday, and stepped back, conscious of the role women played in his culture. Ruby hadn't taken the information at all well and was no doubt planning some feminist enlightening activities should the Japanese plan to relocate to Jeffersonville. Right now, the Jewels had taken the wives to a meeting of the Jeffersonville Garden Club, but Maggie couldn't be in two places at once. And she wanted to be here, with Kyle.

"And you remember Mitchell McCormick," Kyle said, gesturing. He and Maggie had decided that Mitch hadn't needed to be on hand to greet the arriving visitors yesterday, and had assigned him the task of briefing the interpreter.

Behave, Mitch, Maggie pleaded silently. Mitch stood, bowed slightly and spoke a greeting to Mr. Matsuzaka.

In Japanese.

Maggie thought she'd faint. Even Kyle appeared taken by surprise.

Mr. Matsuzaka beamed. So did the other Japanese businessmen with him. Another round of bowing ensued and out came the business cards.

Maggie held her breath. Mitch received the card with both hands, honoring Mr. Matsuzaka. With another burst of Japanese, Mitch quite properly presented his own card to each of the men, then switched to English as he demonstrated his beloved computers.

After the demonstration, Maggie hung back to confront Mitch. "I didn't know you spoke Japanese," she whispered.

"I've been studying on my own. No offense, Mags, but I figured it would be more useful than learning how to drink tea," he replied. "While we were waiting, I practiced with the interpreter. I thought it would be a nice touch."

Maggie studied him. For the first time, she saw beyond the sulking persona he usually adopted, and encountered the very intelligent man who was Kyle's friend and business partner. The man who had charmed her family. She smiled a wide, genuine smile. "It was a *very* nice touch."

OTHER THAN A FEW minor bobbles, the visit had gone well and tonight was the grand finale—the Dogwood Cherry Blossom Ball.

The Jeffersonville Historical Society was arriving in antebellum southern dress—which meant hooped skirts—and Opal had asked Maggie to wear her debut dress. Without giving it too much thought, Maggie had agreed, because that meant she wouldn't have to take time to shop for a new dress.

As she stared at herself in the mirror in her bedroom, she rethought that decision. She hadn't worn the white dress since her debut at sixteen and she appeared to be considerably more buxom now than she'd been then.

The dress definitely didn't have the same sweetly virginal effect that it had once had.

She was also a tad rusty in hoop maneuvering. Rather than attempt a grand descent in front of an admiring Kyle, Maggie opted to go downstairs early. This turned out to be the correct decision, since she couldn't see her feet.

Maggie was trying to find someplace to stand where she wasn't in danger of knocking over a lamp, when a kimono-clad Opal minced into the foyer. "Oh, Maggie, dear, will you sew on my obi? I just need a few stitches here and there. It won't stay put at my waist."

Maggie blinked at the vision of her barrel-shaped great-aunt in a fuchsia kimono. Opal's white hair was piled on top of her head and secured with chopsticks from which tiny paper lanterns dangled. "Where—" Maggie had been going to ask where Opal's waist was, but asked instead, "Where do want me to sew your sash?"

"Here, dear." Opal held it in place as Maggie tried to get close enough to sew a few stitches.

This was the vision that greeted Kyle as he arrived several minutes later.

Kyle in evening clothes was a vision himself. He was perfect. Absolutely perfect. From the top of his expertly groomed head to the tips of his shining shoes, Maggie wouldn't change one thing about him.

"Why, Miss Opal, I do believe pink is your color," he greeted her.

"Oh, you!" She dimpled, took the sewing things from Maggie and left, her steps even tinier than before.

"Well, look at you," Kyle said.

"Yes, look at me." Maggie made a face. "Too much?"

Smiling, he shook his head.

"So how do you think everything is going?"

"I don't know. They're hard to read. Mitch is a big hit, though."

No thanks to her, Maggie thought as Ruby and Pearl arrived in the foyer.

"Mr. Stuart." Pearl, attired in a majestic petal-pink brocade, nodded regally.

Maggie's mother, as usual, wore her pink sari, which she also wore to pink teas. Ruby had been very vocal about the expense of the entertainments, and had only been mollified when Pearl offered to give a tea to raise money for a women's shelter in Jeffersonville.

It promised to be a very eclectic evening.

In spite of the overwhelming pressure Kyle must have been under, he was attentively solicitous of Maggie's grandmother, treating her with enough deference that Pearl bestowed on him an approving smile. With Opal, he engaged in mild flirtatious banter, charming the aging southern belle.

But it was with Ruby that he really shone. When Pearl and Opal disappeared to fetch their wraps, Kyle confronted Maggie's mother. "I am aware that you disapprove of tonight's gathering."

"I don't disapprove at all," Ruby stated. "I merely think the money could be better spent elsewhere."

Kyle inclined his head. "We have a difference of opinion.... However, you did draw my attention to the

Atlanta Women's Shelter. Would it make you feel any better if I tell you that I donated computers to them on your behalf?"

Maggie gasped.

Ruby straightened. "You are attempting to buy my good opinion."

"Absolutely," Kyle said without hesitation. "And not cheaply, either. They're very good computers."

Honestly, the man was trying to bribe her mother. And succeeding, if Ruby's smile was any indication. "Kyle," Maggie warned.

Kyle reached for her hand and squeezed it. Maggie fell silent.

"If you can manage to look like you're having a good time this evening," he told Ruby, "I'll throw in lessons on how to use the computers."

Maggie had not covered bribery in her business-etiquette seminar. Perhaps it was a good thing, since she would have assumed that an affronted look would be the correct response. Certainly not the calculating expression her mother wore as she considered Kyle's offer.

He waited, smiling persuasively.

Ruby's smile widened.

Her mother was *smiling*. Her mother had dimples. Her mother was still a handsome woman, Maggie noted in surprise.

"Ms. Jefferson?" Kyle offered his elbow.

"You may call me Ruby," Maggie's mother said as she tossed the end of her pink sari over her shoulder and tucked her hand around his arm.

Of course, by rights, he should be escorting the two eldest Jefferson women, but Opal had emerged with her wrap and had excitedly stepped out onto the porch.

"That's not the funeral-parlor limousine!" She stopped right at the edge of the porch stairs, forcing everyone behind her to stop also.

Parked at the end of the sidewalk, a long steel-gray car gleamed in the twilight.

Maggie had been concentrating on her hoops and hadn't noticed that it wasn't the black funeral-parlor limousine.

"No, that isn't the funeral-parlor limousine," Kyle said, clearly puzzled.

"No one's getting married this evening—I checked," Opal whispered.

"Is Forest Lawn's car...in use?" Pearl asked delicately.

They were all silent, waiting for Kyle's reply.

"I—I don't know." He looked at Maggie.

She enlightened him. "Jeffersonville only has one limousine."

"Ah." Kyle gestured for the ladies to proceed onward. "I hired this car in Atlanta."

Opal and Pearl exhaled in relief.

"How *thoughtful* of you, Kyle," simpered Ruby.

Her mother was imitating Opal. Maggie's mouth dropped open in astonishment.

In spite of the spacious interior of the car, they were crowded. This was largely due to the yards and yards of net and hoops in Maggie's debut dress.

She wished she hadn't worn it. It *was* too much, though other than two bridesmaids' dresses, it was the only appropriate garment she owned.

Maggie was so preoccupied with her discomfort—and batting down her pillowy dress—that she failed to appreciate Kyle's charming banter until they had arrived at the Jeffersonville Country Club.

With arch looks at both Kyle and Maggie, Pearl and Opal swept into the club, sweeping Ruby right along with them.

Maggie was still in the car, trying to find a way to maneuver herself out. On the one prior occasion she'd worn this dress, she'd changed into it at the club. She couldn't see her feet and had no idea if all the layers of fabric were cleared out of the way, or if the heel of her shoe would catch on one layer and either trip her or tear her dress.

Kyle offered her a hand, but she hesitated. "I'm not quite ready...."

In the end, it took both the driver and Kyle to extricate a completely mortified Maggie. Her face was on fire and she could feel herself perspiring. She avoided looking at Kyle by checking to see that all layers of her stupid dress were where they were supposed to be.

At last she mustered a polite smile and turned to find him regarding her steadily, an arrested expression on his face.

"When I was little," he said in a quiet voice, "my mother used to read me fairy tales. Being a boy, the dragons and ogres and evil magicians appealed to me. I could picture them so clearly, but I was always a bit vague on the fairy princesses. I mean, what kind of girl could be worth fighting a dragon for?"

"Usually a girl with a rich father."

Kyle grinned. "Anyway, I thought she must have been pretty dumb to go and get herself kidnapped by a dragon."

"She probably tripped on her dress," Maggie muttered.

Kyle chuckled. "Ah, but Maggie, it wasn't until I saw you this evening that I fully understood why those knights and princes and all-around good guys went after the dragons." He shoved his hands into his pockets, spoiling the elegant lines of his clothes.

Maggie felt her heart catch. Maybe her dress wasn't so bad, after all.

"You look just like a fairy princess should look." Kyle stepped closer. "And now, whenever I think of one, I'll think of you."

In that moment, Maggie *felt* like a fairy princess—light and fragile and beautiful.

All the trouble she'd had with this ridiculous dress was worth it to see that expression on Kyle's face. It was a romantic you're-the-woman-of-my-dreams sort of expression. Exactly the sort of expression men got before they proposed—or so she'd heard. Maybe tonight she'd find out for sure.

"Shall we?" Kyle gestured toward the doors. "I feel like slaying a dragon or two."

Maggie floated toward him, taking his arm. "I hope that won't be necessary, but if it is, I think you're right for the part."

"THE CHERRY BLOSSOMS are a nice touch," Kyle murmured as he and Maggie mingled with the Jeffersonville elite. The Dogwood Cherry Blossom Ball was in full swing.

"Opal's idea," Maggie said, nodding a greeting to the mayor's wife. "She thought mixing them with the Georgia dogwood would be a subtle hint."

"Subtle? There hasn't been anything subtle about this entire weekend. Matsuzaka is in no doubt that he and his people will be welcomed here." He chuckled. "You, Maggie, come from a formidable family."

She *did* come from a strong family, Maggie thought, her gaze drawn to the group of matrons from where her grandmother unobtrusively, but efficiently, directed the course of the evening. Opal flitted from group to group, making sure no one was left out. Ruby, accompanied by Mitch, was apparently talking computers with a clump of Stuart people, who actually appeared to be enjoying themselves.

The Jewels were shining tonight.

Seeing how they'd risen to the challenge made Maggie realize that she shouldn't have tried to keep their financial problems from them. Once the situation had been clearly and thoroughly explained to them, they'd proved amazingly adaptable.

Even now they were setting up charm-school classes in their home. Maggie, thanks to Kyle's effusive recommendations, had been contacted by several companies, including her former employer, Harlan Edwards of Drake Office Supply, to conduct seminars like the ones she'd held for Kyle.

Now, if only… She gazed at the man standing next to her, letting all the love in her heart show in her eyes.

Kyle cleared his throat. "Let's dance." His eyes never leaving hers, he slipped his arm around her waist and began to move.

The music receded, the crowd faded away. Maggie forgot all about the Jewels and the Japanese. There was only Kyle and the way she felt in his arms.

Maggie had no idea how long she and Kyle were lost in their own world. She didn't care, either.

"Kyle? Maggie?" Mitch appeared beside them.

They jolted to a stop. "What is it?" Kyle shot Mitch an irritated glance.

"Uh, Maggie's mom sent me over here to cut in."

His mouth a straight line, Kyle stepped aside.

Maggie stared across the dance floor to a stern-faced Ruby, who jerked her head toward the knot of Japanese surrounding Opal and Pearl.

Mitch frowned.

"Well?" Kyle gestured. "Go ahead."

"I have to wait until I get the count."

"It's okay, Mitch." Maggie patted his arm. "I think Mama is trying to tell us we're neglecting our duties."

He looked so relieved, she laughed.

"She's right," Kyle acknowledged with a rueful grin as he steered Maggie to the edge of the dance floor.

"And are all your people from Tokyo, Mr. Matsuzaka?" Maggie heard Pearl inquire.

Oh, no. Her grandmother was grilling Mr. Matsuzaka. Maggie searched his face for signs of offense. He appeared reserved, but not angry. But then again, he wouldn't allow his anger to show, would he?

Worried that she should intervene, Maggie gripped Kyle's hand. To her surprise, he patted her arm reassuringly. "Listen," he whispered. "Matsuzaka's speaking of his ancestors."

As Mr. Matsuzaka spoke, Pearl and Opal, lanterns quivering, nodded, obviously concentrating.

Maggie relaxed her hold on Kyle's hand and listened.

"It's been a long trip for you and I know you're looking forward to returning to your families," Pearl said after everyone had tired of exploring bloodlines. "Are you all flying directly home tomorrow?"

"Some of my associates will be returning to San Francisco and from there, to Tokyo," Mr. Matsuzaka said. "However, I am to visit my niece. She is attending one of your universities and will not be able to travel home for many months."

"How nice you can see her, then," murmured Opal.

"And which university is that?" Pearl asked as Maggie had known she would.

"Sophie Newcomb College."

"Oh, in New Orleans!" Opal and Pearl beamed at each other.

Maggie grinned. She should have known her grandmother and great-aunt would eventually find common ground, even conversing with a man whose home was halfway around the world.

"Doesn't Martha Jane's granddaughter go to Sophie

Newcomb?" Pearl mused aloud. "I wonder if she knows your niece."

"Martha Jane's right over there talking to Judge Davis's wife," Opal said.

Maggie didn't know how they managed it, but with merely a look, a raised eyebrow and a slight tilting of the head, Martha Jane was summoned to Pearl and Opal's side.

As they introduced her to Mr. Matsuzaka, Maggie whispered to Kyle, "Should we rescue him now?"

Kyle shook his head. "They seem to be getting along."

"Mr. Matsuzaka's niece attends Sophie Newcomb and I told him Rebecca Ann did, too," Pearl informed Martha Jane. "I wonder if they know each other?"

Martha Jane gasped and clapped her hands together. "Is that darlin' Michiko your niece?"

"Yes!" A surprised Mr. Matsuzaka nodded and beamed. "Yes!"

"Why, isn't it a small world! Michiko and Rebecca Ann live in the same dormitory," Martha Jane told him. To Pearl and Opal she said, "I met Michiko when she and Rebecca Ann came to Savannah over spring break." She turned back to Mr. Matsuzaka. "I was visiting my daughter, Susie."

"Michiko spoke of your family's great kindness to her during her visit."

"Well, she's just a precious girl," Martha Jane pronounced.

"She sounds perfectly lovely," Pearl said, thus bestowing Jeffersonville society's seal of approval on Mr.

Matsuzaka's niece. "And it's so nice that we could meet some of her family."

Maggie heard Kyle chuckle. "I don't believe it," he murmured.

"Oh, I do," she said.

"You know," he said, nudging her away from the group, "I think southern women could rule the world."

"And don't you forget it." She glanced around the room and found that all visitors were deep in conversation. Even Mitch, over by the punch bowl, was talking intently to the interpreter—who had turned out to be a female graduate student.

Kyle touched her arm. "Let's duck outside for a few minutes. I haven't been alone with you for days."

This was it. She knew it in her heart of hearts.

But as they crossed the dance floor, Kyle was hailed by one of his partners and he and Maggie separated.

Feeling tired all at once, she wandered around the perimeter of the room, eavesdropping on conversations.

Pearl was involved in a discussion of gardening, one of her passions. Opal was discussing movies. Ruby... Maggie was suddenly concerned about her mother. Ruby had that look on her face that she got whenever she was expounding on the subject most dear to her heart: the plight of women.

"Yes, I just found that site," her mother was saying. "I'm downloading the information right now." She laughed. "It's so difficult to find a block of time when the phone isn't in use."

The Internet. Her mother was discussing the Internet.

AT LAST, the evening was over.

Pearl and Opal were seeing to the packaging of leftovers and the last Maggie had seen of her mother, Ruby was directing traffic outside the club.

Kyle had escorted their visitors to the Jeffersonville Inn and would be coming back in the car for Maggie and her family. More tired than she'd ever been in her life, Maggie sat, her skirt billowing around her.

Kyle returned after the musicians had packed their instruments and equipment. He walked purposefully across the ballroom floor to stop in front of her.

Bowing, he held out his hand. "Miss Jefferson, I believe we never got to finish our dance."

Her tiredness vanished as Kyle swept her into his arms and waltzed, humming tunelessly. "Maggie, I think we're in," he murmured in her ear. "Matsuzaka couldn't stop talking about tonight and he's practically ready to adopt Mitch. All the bigwigs in town were here and Matsuzaka feels it's a sign of my good standing in the community. But it's a sign of your grandmother's good standing and I know it. I don't know how I'll ever be able to thank her."

By proposing to her granddaughter so she can plan an obscenely huge wedding.

But Kyle kissed Maggie gently, then rested her head on his shoulder.

I don't care if the Japanese come here or not. I just want to be with you forever.

Maggie waited for him to tell her he felt the same way, but he didn't.

I love you. He could say that at least, couldn't he?

Apparently not.

As she and Kyle drifted around the room, Maggie told herself that he was waiting to hear the outcome of the visit before discussing a future with her.

She tried not to feel disappointed after the success of the evening. After all, she'd waited for weeks. She could wait a few days longer.

11

MAGGIE DIDN'T MIND waiting, but not hearing from Kyle at all was something else entirely.

Now that the business-etiquette seminars were over and the Japanese had gone home, she had no excuse to go over to the Stuart Computers building.

When she hadn't heard from him by Tuesday, Maggie decided she'd call him, but didn't. He should call her. The flowers he'd sent to the Jewels didn't count.

Maggie decided that he was waiting until he had news before calling her, but she was still miffed.

She was surprisingly busy, though, working on handouts for her week-long seminar at Drake Office Supply. She was also making flyers and announcements to send to other businesses in the area. The Jewels were occupied with setting up classes for the Jefferson School of Charm.

Tea was back on the daily schedule and Maggie found herself looking forward to the break. Maybe Kyle would even drop in.

"Have you spoken with Mr. Stuart, Magnolia?" Pearl picked a yellowing leaf from the huge floral arrangement he'd sent.

Three pairs of eyes regarded her. "Not yet, but I'm sure I'll hear from him soon."

Three pairs of eyes looked away. Ruby's returned to the computer manuals which now accompanied her to tea. Pearl examined the floral arrangement for more dying leaves. Opal took a plate of lemon cookies and a glass of tea with her to watch television.

"He *will* call," Maggie felt compelled to say.

"Of course, dear." Her grandmother frowned at the silver serving tray and its greatly reduced number of lemon cookies. "Cookie, Magnolia?"

Maggie reached for a cookie, but by the time she brought it to her mouth the lemon odor seemed overwhelming. Her stomach rebelled. Feeling faint, she set the cookie on a napkin.

"Maggie?" Ruby stared at her in concern.

"I'm—I'm tired." She smiled to reassure them, though she really didn't feel well. "I think I'll go lie down."

She was aware of the whispering behind her, but didn't care. She knew what they were saying and Kyle was *not* like their men. He wasn't.

So why hadn't he called her?

WHEN SHE HADN'T HEARD from him by Wednesday afternoon, Maggie was almost too embarrassed to go to tea. She'd avoided everyone all day, which had been easy since they'd spent most of it upstairs doing who knew what. It sounded as if they were moving furniture, but why, Maggie had no idea.

At tea, Maggie saw that Ruby's computer books were gone and she was beginning a new quilt. Pastel blocks were laid out on the end of the sofa table and

Ruby was cutting ducks and bunnies out of pink, yellow, blue and green gingham.

A baby quilt. Maggie smiled and slid into her place. "Who's having a baby, Mama?" Maybe they'd forget to ask her about Kyle.

Ruby eyed her over the tops of the half glasses she'd recently taken to wearing. "How are you feeling this afternoon, Maggie?"

"Tired," she answered truthfully. "I must be coming down with something."

Ruby held her gaze, then returned to her ducks.

Pearl arrived, carrying the tea things, followed by Opal with the lemon cookies.

Maggie swallowed dryly. Lemon cookies did not have the appeal for her that they once did.

"And how are you today, Magnolia?" Pearl scooted over some of Ruby's squares and set the tea tray on the table.

"Fine," Maggie answered, with an edge to her voice. She wished they'd stop asking her how she felt all the time.

She reached for a glass of iced tea, but Pearl shook her head.

"This one is for you, dear." Her grandmother handed her a glass that was considerably paler than the rest. "Herbal tea. It's best to cut back on caffeine now."

Herbal tea? "Frankly, I'm so tired, I could use a shot of caffeine." Maybe if she could choke down a lemon cookie, the sugar would give her a lift. Maggie reached for one and stopped, her fingers poised above the plate.

Nestled among the lemon cookies were soda crackers. "I bought the unsalted kind," Opal said. "They'll be better for your stomach."

Maggie jerked her hand away. They thought... "No," she said very firmly.

They looked at her.

"No," she said again.

"We've already moved the crib into the room next to yours, Maggie." Opal patted her hand.

"You'll want to set up an appointment with Dr. Harrison," Pearl advised. "Dr. Purvis, himself, trained him. Dr. Purvis delivered you and your mother, you know."

Maggie stood. "No. It's...it's impossible."

"But Maggie...he has blue eyes," Opal said, as if that explained everything.

Maggie stalked out of the room. At the door, she turned and delivered one last and insistent, "No!"

YES.

Maggie hadn't wanted to use the home pregnancy test that one of her thoughtful but wrongheaded relatives had left on her bed, but she'd decided to, just to prove them wrong.

Instead, she was standing in the bathroom staring at a stick with a big red plus.

"No!" The word echoed around the bathroom and then Maggie threw up.

"MR. MATSUZAKA, I'm sure it will be a most profitable relationship for us both." After a few more pleasantries, Kyle carefully, gently and slowly cradled the phone.

"Yes! Yes, yes, yes!" He punched his fist into the air.

Then he called Maggie. Tonight, they were going to celebrate.

"Maggie?"

"One moment, Mr. Stuart." Kyle drummed his fingers on his desk until he heard approaching footsteps.

"Hello?" The word was crisply professional, but he ignored the tone. She'd warm up when she heard the news.

"Maggie—we did it!"

"Yes, we certainly did."

Kyle hesitated, then continued, "The Japanese are coming to Jeffersonville. I've spent the last four days faxing and phoning and having conferences at strange hours and just this minute, Mr. Matsuzaka gave me the news." He stopped to breathe. "You're the only other person who knows."

"Oh, Kyle." Her voice was considerably warmer. "Oh, Kyyyyyllllle!" And she started sobbing.

Kyle was taken aback. But of course she would have been under as much strain as he'd been. "Maggie, don't cry. It's good news. Listen, I want to see you tonight...pick you up at—" Kyle would have to announce the news to his staff. Who knew how long he'd be. "Can you be at the penthouse at seven? I'm going to be tied up in meetings for the rest of the day, but I'll make it a point to get away then."

The sobs quieted. "Okay. I...just got a little emotional."

"Believe me, I got emotional, too." He exhaled as the news and what it meant truly registered. "Oh, Maggie, I need you so much."

"Kyle...I need you, too."

IT WAS EIGHT O'CLOCK before Kyle arrived at the penthouse. Maggie had fallen asleep on the couch, but she heard him come in.

"Hey, Maggie. Sorry I'm late." He ripped off his tie as he strode across the room and planted a quick kiss on her forehead. "This has been some day."

"Yes, it has." And it wasn't over yet.

Kyle took off his shoes and collapsed on the couch beside her. Though he was obviously tired, he was more animated than Maggie had ever seen him, telling her about everyone's reaction to the news.

He didn't seem to notice that she was quieter than usual and she decided to let him talk himself out. There would be plenty more to talk about later.

She was going to give him a chance to tell her he loved her before telling him about the baby.

She was going to give him a chance to propose before she told him about the baby.

And tonight was the night. She just knew it.

Maggie curled her feet under her on the leather couch as Kyle talked on and on, describing every step that had led to the Japanese agreement.

And then he described—in excruciating technical detail—exactly how this wonderful chip would work in his computers. Then he talked about building the computers. Then he talked about marketing the computers.

Maggie listened to every word, waiting to hear where she fit in this wonderful future he described.

"I can't believe it's really happening." He threw his head back on the couch and stared at the ceiling. "And I couldn't have done it without you." Turning to face her, Kyle reached over and took her hand. "Thanks."

Maggie felt tears sting her eyes. He was about to tell her he loved her and ask her to marry him. She wanted to remember this moment for the rest of her life.

He looked so serious, but this was a serious moment.

He squeezed her hand. "I'm going to miss you more than I can ever say."

"M-miss me?"

"That's the only bad part about this whole deal. I've got to go to Japan for a year or eighteen months, and set up a distribution system like I've got here. Mr. Matsuzaka will run things here until I get back."

"You're going to Japan?" Maggie repeated dully as the blood began pounding in her ears.

He nodded. "Yeah. But I'll—"

"You're going to leave me and go to *Japan?*"

"I have to, Maggie. You knew that was always a possibility."

No, she hadn't known. Maggie felt sick, really sick. She stood. "You mean I've worked and worked just so you could leave?"

"I'm not leaving forever." He stood, too, and held her shoulders. "And we still have a week or two together before I have to go." He leaned down to kiss her.

Maggie jerked away. "A *week*?"

"Maggie." Kyle turned her to face him. "I know it's a long time, but—"

"You're leaving me!" She looked around for something to throw, but Kyle didn't have any pillows. "I can't believe you're leaving me! I can't believe it happened to me. You're just like the others."

"Maggie," he pleaded, but she'd quit listening. He was leaving. There was nothing more to be said.

She grabbed her purse and ran out the door, ignoring Kyle's shouts.

He was leaving. Soon. Her love hadn't been enough—or had it been too much?

She got in her grandmother's old pink car and gunned the engine. Minutes later, she was turning toward the Jefferson house on Jefferson Boulevard where she would raise the child of the blue-eyed Yankee who'd abandoned her.

Just like all the women in the Jefferson family.

"I'M NOT AT HOME to Mr. Stuart," Maggie announced at teatime several days later.

The Jewels all knew that Kyle was off to Japan.

"But he said he'd be back, right, Maggie?" Opal looked at her anxiously.

Maggie bit into a cracker. "That's what they all said."

"You didn't tell him about the baby." Ruby was appliquéing pink gingham rabbits on green squares to-day.

"I didn't think I was supposed to," Maggie said. "If I'm going to follow the tradition, I'm going to follow it exactly."

After that, the Jewels learned not to talk to her about Kyle anymore.

For her part, Maggie docilely presented herself each day for tea. Most of her waking hours were occupied in trying to figure out how she came to be in the situation she'd dreaded most and what she could do about it.

The Jewels tried to recruit her for charm-school duty, but Maggie declined. She'd better work to establish her protocol consulting business now, before the baby came. There would be no trust fund to support them as there had been when her mother had returned home to have Maggie.

Oddly enough, Maggie felt closer to the three women than she ever had. She'd loved and lost. She understood them now.

She also wondered which brand of condoms had failed. The only ones she could eliminate for certain were the animal-print ones, since they'd never gotten around to using those.

The day before Kyle was to leave, there was a knock on the door during tea.

Maggie wasn't at all surprised to hear his voice at the door. She *was* surprised that he was angry enough to push past a fluttering Opal.

"Why the *hell* won't you talk to me!" he thundered

without regard to the sensibilities of Maggie's relatives.

"I have nothing to say to you," Maggie replied.

"You're going to let me leave for Japan without even saying goodbye?"

"Goodbye," she said.

He stood there, all flushed and heart-breakingly handsome. And Maggie's traitorous heart still warmed.

The Jewels listened avidly.

"I don't get it. What happened?"

Maggie didn't answer, but she glared at the older women, telepathically swearing them to silence.

Ruby cleared her throat. Kyle glanced at her and she smoothed the fabric she was quilting, turning it so he could see the bunny.

"We're making new curtains for the room next to Maggie's," Pearl said. She held up two swatches. One was pink and white with little lambs, the other had characters from Mother Goose dancing across a yellow background. "Which do you prefer?"

Maggie glared at her grandmother.

"Lemon cookie, Mr. Stuart?" Opal offered him the plate with the crackers and cookies on it. "Of course, if your tummy is queasy like Maggie's is these days, you may prefer a cracker."

Maggie glared at her great-aunt.

. In the heavy silence, Kyle murmured something polite and took a cookie, bit into it, chewed slowly, then swallowed. Instead of taking another bite, he stared at the plate, his eyes widening. He glanced at Maggie, then his gaze swept the crackers, the curtain material and Ruby's quilt.

Maggie felt her face heat and knew it had turned a telltale red.

"Maggie?" He looked thunderstruck.

"Sit down, Mr. Stuart." Opal led him to a chair and tugged on his arm until he sat. "You've had a shock."

"Maggie?"

She would admit nothing. Let him go to Japan and wonder. She sent a warning glare around the room.

"Maggie, say something."

"Bon voyage."

"Maggie, I love you!"

He must feel really guilty to have said that in front of her family. Too bad for him they'd heard it all before. They wouldn't be impressed.

"I was trying to tell you the other night, but you ran out."

"No, *you're* the one who's running."

"I— If you'd told me—" He broke off and rubbed his hand over the back of his neck. "And that's why you didn't." Leaping out of his chair, he crossed the room and knelt by hers. "Maggie, this changes everything."

"You're not kidding."

"I've still got to go to Japan tomorrow, but I'll work something out. It'll take me a couple of weeks, but I'll be back." He took her hands. "I love you, Maggie. I want us to get married. You'll marry me, won't you, Maggie?"

She could hear sniffing. Didn't the Jewels ever learn?

This was all for show. He wasn't coming back. "Ask me again in a couple of weeks."

"BUT MAGGIE, you simply must decide on your wedding colors. We don't want to delay *too* long." Opal spread out her bridal magazines, trying to tempt Maggie.

She sipped her herbal tea. "I don't know why you're going to all this trouble. He's not coming back."

"I'm inclined to believe he is, Magnolia." Pearl was looking at menus from the Jeffersonville Country Club, as though she hadn't already memorized them for the Japanese extravaganza.

"He's a blue-eyed Yankee. They never come back."

The women stilled.

"In light of your delicate condition, I shall overlook your outburst," Pearl said.

Maggie felt anything but delicate. She was living on soda crackers and tea.

"If I use a script font, I can print Maggie's wedding invitations on the laser printer." Ruby held up a sample of a formal white invitation.

"I think not. This will be a Jefferson wedding and the invitations will be engraved," Pearl pronounced. "I see no reason why you can't print up the menu, though, Ruby," she compromised, something that would have been unheard of a few weeks ago.

"You're wasting your time," Maggie said. She'd said it before and no one had listened to her. They weren't listening now, either.

Wedding plans had been the sole topic of conversation at tea for the endless days since Kyle had left.

They actually thought he'd be back.

He'd called twice, or so they said, but Maggie had been asleep both times and he'd refused to let them wake her.

They were probably making it all up.

"Now, Maggie, if you don't choose your colors today, then we'll choose them for you."

"Fine. I choose orange and purple. If I'm going to feel sick, then I want everyone else to feel sick, too."

Amid all the tongue-clucking, they almost missed the tapping at the door.

"Magnolia," Pearl said, "it appears we have a visitor."

Ruby cleared away her paper samples and Opal arranged herself so her best side showed.

"One of the charm-school students probably forgot something," Maggie told them.

Her grandmother nodded her toward the door.

Through the lace curtains, Maggie saw a smudge of red.

Kyle's car.

Then she opened the door and there he was.

"Hello, Maggie." He grinned crookedly. "I'm back. Am I too late for tea?"

Heedless of the packages in his arms, Maggie flung herself at him. "Are you back for good?"

"Yes. I told you I was coming back."

"I know, but...so did the others." She gestured to the back parlor, where the Jewels were waiting.

"May I come in?" Kyle asked.

Maggie, her heart feeling as though it were about to burst, led Kyle to the tea tableau.

"Mr. Stuart," Pearl said, heavy satisfaction sounding in her voice. "Welcome back."

"I brought something for you all." After checking the labels, he handed a soft package to each of the Jewels.

Opal ripped hers open first and withdrew a length of vibrant pink silk. There was purple for Pearl and a ruby red for Ruby. Amid the pleased exclamations, Kyle said, "I thought you could have dresses made up in time for the wedding. How are the plans going, by the way?"

Pearl carefully folded her length of silk. "Plans are proceeding in spite of Magnolia's lack of cooperation."

Kyle looked down at her. "I think I can speed things along here."

He reached into his pocket and withdrew a ring box. There was a hushed silence as he dropped to one knee in front of Maggie. "Magnolia Blossom Jefferson, will you be my wife?"

He'd come back, just as he'd said he would. And now he was asking her to marry him, just as she'd told him to.

Maggie was too emotional to speak, but she could nod, and nod she did.

Opal burst into tears. "This is better than TV!"

Kyle stood and opened the ring box. "I picked this out in Japan. It's a pearl," he said. "Like your name. Maggie."

Ruby turned to her mother. "You see?" Tears streamed down her face. "I told you it meant Pearl."

Maggie loved him for the symbolism he'd given her ring. "It's beautiful," she whispered, and held out her hand.

Pearl maintained a stoic expression until the enormous ring was on Maggie's finger, thus signifying an official engagement for her granddaughter. Then she covered her eyes and wept silently.

"I'm going to borrow Maggie for a bit," Kyle said, visibly uncomfortable in a room of weeping women.

Three lace-edged hankies waved them out the door.

Maggie was teary-eyed herself. He'd come back to her. They were going to be married.

It wasn't until they were in the car and driving past the statue of LaRue Jefferson in Jefferson Square that Maggie thought to ask how Kyle was able to get out of his obligations in Japan.

"Mitch is going in my place."

"*Mitch?*"

Kyle nodded. "He's been dating that interpreter and I gather he's making tremendous progress in Japanese. He's looking forward to going to Japan, especially since she'll be spending the rest of the summer there."

Maggie shook her head in wonder.

Instead of turning into the parking lot, they drove right on past the Stuart building. "Where are we going?" she asked.

"I've put in a bid on a house," he said, surprising her.

Maggie tried to imagine what kind of house Kyle

would buy and why he'd buy one without her. "How much farther?"

"Ten minutes or so," he said, turning off the main road and smiling at her reassuringly.

"Did you buy land, or something?" Maggie asked, feeling uncertain. "There's nothing out here but the old Garthwhiddle place and that's been shut up for years—ever since Salina Garthwhiddle died."

"Not anymore." Kyle settled back and propped his elbow on the window ledge.

Maggie's eyes widened. "Kyle—you didn't buy the old Garthwhiddle home?"

Kyle grinned.

"It's a wreck!"

At that moment, they emerged from the bower of trees. The tires crunched as Kyle turned his car off the public road and onto an overgrown private one.

"You can still get your money back, can't you?" Maggie gritted her teeth as the car jounced along the road.

"Why would I want to do that?" he asked, stopping at an iron gate. "Be back in a minute."

He grabbed a flashlight, jumped out of the car and approached the gate.

Maggie saw him reach into his pocket. "He's got a key," she moaned. If things had progressed that far, he was serious.

"You haven't signed anything yet, have you?" she asked when he returned and drove the car through the gate. The driveway was almost nonexistent.

"Shh."

Maggie shushed.

"Now just look at that." He pointed toward a great white hulk with dark windows.

In the growing twilight, the old plantation-style house gleamed against the darkening sky. The weathered paint appeared fresh and the tangled yard wasn't so noticeable.

But this was in the forgiving light of evening. Maggie had seen the house in the harsh reality of daylight.

Kyle pulled to a stop and turned off the engine. They sat quietly as Maggie struggled for something to say.

"It's awfully big, isn't it?" she said finally.

"*Gracious* is the word I prefer." Kyle propped his arms over the steering wheel and gazed at the house. "And it isn't as big as a regular plantation home. This one was built during the Reconstruction. It's a scaled-down version of Dogwood Hill, the Garthwhiddle plantation house that was burned—"

"I know the history of the house," Maggie inserted dryly. "What I don't know is what you intend to do with it."

"We're going to fix it up and live in it. This is part of Jeffersonville's past. We need to preserve it."

"Out with the old, in with the new."

"Maggie, Maggie," he chastised her, shaking his head. "Doesn't it speak to you?"

Maggie cupped her hand around her ear. "Yes...it's saying, 'dry rot...termites...leaky plumbing...inadequate wiring—'"

"Magnolia Blossom Jefferson." Kyle drawled her entire name. "Of all people, I thought *you* would fall in love with this place." He shook his head, making little tsking noises.

"This place has got 'money-pit' written all over it."

"Aren't you glad you're marrying a man with money?"

She eyed him. Surely he didn't think... "I love you. I would have married you even if you didn't have money." She wanted him to understand that she was not marrying him out of desperation. "I would have married you even if you'd lost your business and had to leave Jeffersonville. And because I love you, I guess I'll marry you even though you own a run-down house."

He laughed and put his arm around her. "It's not going to stay that way. Hey, I'm marrying Maggie Jefferson of the Jeffersonville Jeffersons. I won't have anybody saying she married down."

"No, they'll be talking about something else," she said wryly.

Kyle placed his hand over her stomach. "We haven't talked much about the baby," he said quietly. "I'm very happy about Junior, here. I thought about him and becoming a father every day I was gone. He's part me and part you. He's what our love made, Maggie."

"I've been so afraid that you..." She couldn't finish.

"Oh, no. Never." He kissed her temple. "You know, this baby beat incredible odds. He's going to be tough."

"It's changed so much for you, though."

"And a good thing, too. Without him, I might have

actually stayed in Japan and then I would have lost you."

"Why do you keep calling the baby 'he'?"

"Because it's time one of you Jeffersons had a boy."

"I don't know, the female Jefferson tradition is pretty strong."

In the darkness, Kyle's eyes looked particularly blue. "Then that'll be two traditions I'm breaking."

_____Epilogue_____

TIDBITS FROM the *Jefferson Journal*:

President Suki Matsuzaka announced that the February meeting of the Jeffersonville Garden Club will be a bonsai demonstration at the home of Pearl Jefferson.

Ruby Jefferson, director of the new Jeffersonville Women's Shelter, invites all Jeffersonville residents to an Open House on February 25 from 3:00 to 5:00 p.m.

Mr. and Mrs. Kyle Stuart of Magnolia Hill (formerly Dogwood Hill) proudly announce the birth of their son, Jefferson Onyx Stuart, on February 20th. Mrs. Stuart, the former Magnolia Jefferson, is the great-great-granddaughter of LaRue Jefferson, founder of Jeffersonville. Little Jefferson becomes LaRue Jefferson's first great-great-great-grandchild and the first male Jefferson in four generations. His great-grandmother, local civic leader Pearl Jefferson, is president of the Jeffersonville Historical Society, immediate past president of the Garden Club and director of the Jeffersonville School of Charm. His great-great-aunt, Opal Jefferson, is an instructor at the Jeffersonville School of Charm and president of numerous soap opera fan clubs. She currently serves as secretary of the Jeffersonville Drama Guild. His grandmother is local activist Ruby Jefferson, director of the Jeffersonville Women's Shelter.

Mr. Stuart is a local businessman.

**Temptation keeps turning up
the heat with**

**Look for these bold, provocative,
ultra-sexy books!**

Available in November:

SCANDALIZED! by Lori Foster

Tony Austin wanted a baby, but he didn't want a wife.
Olivia Anderson wanted a lover, but not a husband. It
should have been the perfect coupling, but sometimes
the best-laid plans don't quite work out. Sometimes
passion can't be controlled....

BLAZE! Red-hot reads from Temptation!

Take 4 bestselling love stories FREE

Plus get a FREE surprise gift!

Special Limited-time Offer

Mail to Harlequin Reader Service®

3010 Walden Avenue
P.O. Box 1867
Buffalo, N.Y. 14240-1867

YES! Please send me 4 free Harlequin Temptation® novels and my free surprise gift. Then send me 4 brand-new novels every month, which I will receive before they appear in bookstores. Bill me at the low price of $2.90 each plus 25¢ delivery and applicable sales tax, if any.* That's the complete price and a savings of over 10% off the cover prices—quite a bargain! I understand that accepting the books and gift places me under no obligation ever to buy any books. I can always return a shipment and cancel at any time. Even if I never buy another book from Harlequin, the 4 free books and the surprise gift are mine to keep forever.

142 BPA A3UP

Name	(PLEASE PRINT)	
Address	Apt. No.	
City	State	Zip

This offer is limited to one order per household and not valid to present Harlequin Temptation® subscribers. *Terms and prices are subject to change without notice. Sales tax applicable in N.Y.

UTEMP-696 ©1990 Harlequin Enterprises Limited

DELTA JUSTICE

A family dynasty of law and order is shattered by a mysterious crime of passion.

Don't miss the second Delta Justice book as the mystery unfolds in:

Letters, Lies and Alibis
by Sandy Steen

Rancher Travis Hardin is determined to right a sixty-year wrong and wreak vengeance on the Delacroix. But he hadn't intended to fall in love doing it. Was his desire for Shelby greater than his need to destroy her family?

Lawyer Shelby Delacroix never does anything halfway. She is passionate about life, her work...and Travis. Lost in a romantic haze, Shelby encourages him to join her in unearthing the Delacroix family secrets. Little does she suspect that Travis is keeping a few secrets of his own....

Available in October
wherever Harlequin books are sold.

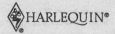

HARLEQUIN®

Look us up on-line at: http://www.romance.net

DJ2

HARLEQUIN® Temptation

Their worlds collided in a torrid night to remember

Kat Kiley was a woman who knew passion but not love. J. P. Harrington was a man who knew love but not passion. They were as different as night and day, except that they both put their lives on the line for their work. Desperate circumstances brought them together, and from that moment on they were joined by destiny—whether they liked it or not.

IT HAPPENED ONE NIGHT

Enjoy #660 *Heart and Soul* by Susan Worth. Available in November 1997.

Sensuous stories from Temptation about heroes and heroines who share a single sizzling night of love.... And damn the consequences!

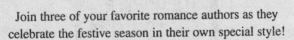

HARLEQUIN WOMEN KNOW ROMANCE WHEN THEY SEE IT.

And they'll see it on **ROMANCE CLASSICS**, the new 24-hour TV channel devoted to romantic movies and original programs like the special **Romantically Speaking—Harlequin™ Goes Prime Time**.

Romantically Speaking—Harlequin™ Goes Prime Time introduces you to many of your favorite romance authors in a program developed exclusively for Harlequin® readers.

Watch for **Romantically Speaking—Harlequin™ Goes Prime Time** beginning in the summer of 1997.

If you're not receiving ROMANCE CLASSICS, call your local cable operator or satellite provider and ask for it today!

ROMANCE
CLASSICS

Escape to the network of your dreams.

See Ingrid Bergman and Gregory Peck in *Spellbound* on Romance Classics.

Free Gift Offer

With a Free Gift proof-of-purchase
from any Harlequin® book, you can receive
a beautiful cubic zirconia pendant.

This stunning marquise-shaped stone is a genuine cubic
zirconia—accented by an 18" gold tone necklace.
(Approximate retail value $19.95)

Send for yours today...
compliments of ✦HARLEQUIN®

To receive your free gift, a cubic zirconia pendant, send us one original proof-of-purchase, photocopies not accepted, from the back of any Harlequin Romance®, Harlequin Presents®, Harlequin Temptation®, Harlequin Superromance®, Harlequin Intrigue®, Harlequin American Romance®, or Harlequin Historicals® title available at your favorite retail outlet, together with the Free Gift Certificate, plus a check or money order for $1.65 U.S./$2.15 CAN. (do not send cash) to cover postage and handling, payable to Harlequin Free Gift Offer. We will send you the specified gift. Allow 6 to 8 weeks for delivery. Offer good until December 31, 1997, or while quantities last. Offer valid in the U.S. and Canada only.

Free Gift Certificate

Name: _____

Address: _____

City: _____ State/Province: _____ Zip/Postal Code: _____

Mail this certificate, one proof-of-purchase and a check or money order for postage and handling to: HARLEQUIN FREE GIFT OFFER 1997. In the U.S.: 3010 Walden Avenue, P.O. Box 9071, Buffalo NY 14269-9057. In Canada: P.O. Box 604, Fort Erie, Ontario L2Z 5X3.

FREE GIFT OFFER   084-KEZ

ONE PROOF-OF-PURCHASE
To collect your fabulous FREE GIFT, a cubic zirconia pendant, you must include this original proof-of-purchase for each gift with the properly completed Free Gift Certificate.

084-KEZR